To William
Thank you for
sharing your book

The Man Under the Bridge

JoEllen Oliver
aka Jillian Wright

Jillian Wright

authorHOUSE®

AuthorHouse™
1663 Liberty Drive, Suite 200
Bloomington, IN 47403
www.authorhouse.com
Phone: 1-800-839-8640

First published by AuthorHouse 4/14/2009

ISBN: 978-1-4389-5669-5 (sc)

Printed in the United States of America
Bloomington, Indiana

This book is printed on acid-free paper.

Table of Contents

Preface

When I was a small girl---maybe five or six----a dirty, ragged, and unshaven man came to the back door of our Cape Cod home in a quiet, middle-class neighborhood. I don't think he said anything; I remember him standing with his hand out. I must have been startled because my mother sought to reassure me, "Don't worry, it's just a tramp. Go see if there's anything left from dinner to give him." In those days, before the word "homeless" became a part of the common vocabulary, there was not the fear and hatred that some people feel toward those individuals today. Neither was there any particular sentiment or pity about these "knights of the road." A handout, if there were leftovers from dinner, was considered the proper response.

As it turned out, we didn't have enough leftovers, so we made a sandwich of cold meat and another of peanut butter and served them on a paper napkin. We put out some iced tea in a jelly jar. My mother was happy to give out food, but not on her good dishes. My brother once got into trouble for carrying lemonade in a crystal goblet to a black man working in the neighbor's yard. This particular neighbor did not give out anything to the poor unless the beggar did some work. In this case, the man was sweating heavily for fifty cents, and the lemonade was much appreciated. But my brother was scolded at home because he didn't serve it in a jelly jar.

To my knowledge, no one asked any of these itinerant beggars how they happened to get in that condition. As the "tramp" sat on the back steps munching his sandwich, I must have asked about how such people came to be, because I remember my grandfather saying, "You don't see many of those folks any more. There used to be a lot of them in the depression." He then went on to tell about how people lost their jobs in the depression, and almost everyone, including himself, was poor. "Most people got jobs again, but some people never got over the depression. "

"And some people just like traveling around on trains with no responsibilities," added my mother.

"Until the railroads cracked down on them," my grandfather responded.

A few years later we moved to a large industrial city. Freeways were just beginning to be built, by-passing some of the older highways. One of the older highways went near our home, and under the bridge lived a man. One Saturday my brother and I and two other teen-agers, feeling adventurous, set out to see the "man under the bridge." The highway was still unsafe for walking and we had to park some distance away. By creeping along the rail and peering over the edge, we could see the top of a tarpaper shack. No one had the courage to get off the side of the road and descend into the gully. I never saw this homeless man, but one of the neighborhood kids claimed to have seen him. "He was going back down into his shack with a bag of groceries. I also saw him with a sack of cans he picked up on the highway. He had white hair and a long beard." We then had a discussion about how the man could afford to buy groceries. We decided he must have earned some change picking up cans. Recycling was not in fashion yet, but people could sometimes get a little money from cans.

There were many rumors about how the man under the bridge came to be there, but most people agreed that he must have been disappointed in love. His sweetheart had married someone else, the story went, and since that time he wanted nothing to do with people. The reason I am telling this story is to emphasize that this man was, if not unique, at least a novelty. At that time I never realized that years later, during the 1980's, hundreds of homeless people would take shelter under the bridges of freeways in that same city.

Still more years passed and I was a young married woman. We were on a tour of New York City. For the most part, the Gray Line Tour was upbeat: the Rockerfeller Center and the Statue of Liberty were my favorite sites. But one of the attractions was a drive through the Bowery. I could never understand why some people thought it was fun to see people lying in doorways and on sidewalks, sometimes covered with their own vomit. Some looked to be already dead. Nevertheless, the Bowery was considered a tourist attraction because of its relatively unique flavor. One saw such sights in only a few locations. Such people were not scattered throughout the landscape. Now all that has changed, and homeless people have become the topic of endless debates and the cause of strong emotions. The public has a love-hate relationship with these people.

Not long ago, my husband Dave and I were attending a conference in Denver. Although it was late spring, the temperature was near freezing. As we walked down the street, we saw a man rummaging through a garbage can, obviously looking for something to eat. He wore jeans but had no shirt or jacket. In the near-freezing temperature, he was naked from the waist up. In retrospect, I realized that I should have tried to call some authorities, in the hope that they would take him to a warm place and feed him. Of course he would have been gone before anyone arrived. At the moment, however, all we could think of to do was to try to give him a twenty. Maybe he could go in a fast food place, or at least buy a shirt.

We walked up to the man. "Sir," I said, "Do you need some money to eat?" His eyes were wild with absolute terror. He looked at me in horror and fled, without the twenty.

This is not an intellectual book about the causes of homelessness, nor is it a book about cures. There are plenty of statistics available to assess the demographic nature of this population. A number of solutions have also been offered, some benevolent and some mean-spirited, depending upon one's political agenda. This is a fictionalized story about some homeless people's perceptions of how they came to be the way they are, and more importantly, how they perceive the meaning of their lives. Their stories are necessarily subjective, told to volunteers at various shelters and agencies serving the homeless. By re-telling their stories, I hope to put a face on the person who has no home, and, as the economy worsens and more people are losing jobs and homes, this population will only become more diverse. The homeless are not a homogenous population. Each is a unique individual.

Wherever You Are, I Will Find You

Some women in shelters have to literally run for their lives. And not only must they run, they must hide. I remember a number of years ago when our very first shelter in this area opened. It was the first place to accept women with children who might be escaping domestic abuse. I read in the paper about the opening, but I was not particularly interested in shelters or the people who might live in them.

At that time, I was a teacher in a rural area. I commuted about 30 miles from our town to teach eighth grade. Every teacher usually has a few students who hang around after class to talk about their lives. Some of these children are just wanting attention from an adult, some are wanting to "butter up" the teacher for a good grade, some need help with an assignment, and some are just friendly kids who are interested in everyone. Benjy was a really verbal kid who liked to talk about everything. Unfortunately, Benjy's written skills were not as good as his oral skills. He was barely passing, so I assumed he was trying to "butter me up," or at least get help, when he started hanging around to talk.

I had sent some of Benjy's written essays home with a note for his mother to sign. I knew Benjy lived with his mother and a stepfather, and I had hoped they might want to help him with homework, so I suggested they drill him on vocabulary and spelling. Benjy was now returning the set of papers with his mother's signature. I checked her signature to be sure it wasn't actually Benjy's writing, and then I saw a faintly scribbled message in pencil. "If I come there-will you help me?" was written just above the signature in the margin..

"What is this about? Who wrote it?" I demanded of Benjy. The other kids had already gone.

"My mom wants to know if you will help her. I'm supposed to tell her what you said," the boy answered.

"Help her with what?" I asked. "Maybe this mom wanted help with her own educational goals, perhaps with reading," I was thinking..

"My step dad beats her," Benjy continued. "Yesterday he dragged her around by the hair and then pounded her head on the cement drive. I wanted to do something terrible to him, but my mom said not to-that I'd just get into trouble."

"How awful!" I gasped. "But I don't see how I can help. You and your mother should call the law to help you."

"The sheriff is my stepfather's brother. He probably wouldn't do anything."

"Wouldn't you know it?" I thought. "In these rural places they may have only one officer of the law, and everybody is related to everybody else."

"Why doesn't your mother leave him?" I wanted to know.

"She doesn't know where to go. She has one sister, but the last time-when she went there, he found her right away. Every day he tells her, 'Don't even think about leaving. Wherever you go, I will find you-and wherever you are, I will kill you.'"

I shuddered. "But then," I thought, "maybe this kid is exaggerating. I need to hear it from the mother herself."

"Tell your mother she needs to come see me about your English grade. Tell her to come by herself. When could she come?"

"She works until four. My step dad picks her up so she doesn't have a chance to run away or anything. He also takes her pay."

I wasn't happy to hear the step dad would probably be coming. But maybe I could figure out how to talk to this woman alone. "Tell her I'll wait until she gets off work."

It was not until Benjy had left and I was on the way home that I thought about the new homeless shelter. Maybe this could be an answer for this mother.

The next day shortly after four, Benjy's mother, Kristine, slipped furtively into my room. I expected to see the husband right behind her. "He's outside in the truck," she said, as though anticipating my question. She spoke in such a low voice I could hardly hear her. "When Benjy gave me your message I asked if I could come see you about his grades, and he said he would bring me here and I could stay 15 minutes. He's right outside so I better get out there before the 15 minutes are up."

"Is it true what your son said-that this man physically abuses you?"

She asked me to take my hand and place it on her head. Under her streaked, gray-brown hair I could feel ridges and bumps. "That's from him pounding my head on the driveway," she said. "Besides that, my neck hurts something fierce from his twisting it around."

"Would you leave him if you had a place to go?" She nodded yes.

I told her about the new shelter in my town. "I could take you there," I offered, "but first I have to find out what the requirements are and if they have room. They may not even take you if you don't live in our county."

I promised to investigate the shelter this very evening, and then we devised a plan to communicate. If I called her house and said that her child failed his spelling test, that meant that the shelter was available. If I said that he needed more help in English, that meant that we would have to think of something else to do.

"If I give you a ride to this shelter in my town," I wanted to know, "how do we keep your husband from following us? How will you even manage to get out of his sight?"

Kristine already had a plan. Even though her husband always drove her to work and picked her up, he could not watch her all the time while she was at work. Across the street from the chicken processing plant where she worked was a small convenience store where employees sometimes went to get cigarettes on their breaks.

"I will wait until about 3:15 when school is out to take my smoking break," she said, "and then I'll run across the street on the pretense of buying cigarettes. You can pick me up outside the store and you will have Benjy in the car. He won't expect me to get off work for another 35 or 40 minutes, and by that time we'll be long gone."

I knew I might be doing something risky. Nowadays teachers are not even allowed to transport students in their cars. In those days there was no rule against it, but I still didn't want people to know that I was helping this child and his mother to escape. I didn't even feel it was safe to tell the principal because he was close friends with the sheriff—and as I had been told, the sheriff was the brother of the abusive husband. All of them went hunting together.

The shelter manager told me I could bring the mother and son the next day, so I called Benjy's home and said, in case Sam, the husband, was listening, that the son needed more work in spelling. "He failed his test but he can take it again tomorrow afternoon," I said.

The next morning, Benjy pulled me to one side before school started and showed me his heavy book bag. Underneath his books was a change of underwear and socks and some toothpaste and other toilet articles

5

for both him and his mother. She could not dare take anything to work for fear of arousing suspicion. She had, however, worn several layers of clothing, according to Benjy. Today was the day.

At three o'clock when students left, some went to buses and some went to cars. Benjy left ahead of me and walked like he was going to the bus. Without telling anyone, he kept walking until he got to my car on the back side of the school. I left separately, slid quickly into the seat and drove off. I don't know if anyone noticed our departure. I had already signed out early, pleading a doctor's appointment. Fortunately, most of the teachers were inside because we weren't supposed to leave until four.

When we approached the small convenience store, Benjy's mom was standing outside smoking a cigarette. Her hands were trembling. Obviously she was as nervous as I was. "What kind of truck does your husband drive?" I asked.

"Dark green. Chevrolet." I looked in the rear view mirror all the way, the man's words ringing in my ears: "Wherever you go, I will find you-and wherever you are, I will kill you."

Once safely inside the shelter, with no dark green truck following us, I breathed a sigh of relief. This was my first experience with being inside a homeless shelter, which was, surprisingly, rather pleasant and, well-almost home-like. My student and his mother were among the first residents. Years later I would do counseling there - with all kinds of residents.

The next day the sheriff came into my classroom. "Is Benjamin Crawford here?" he demanded. I pretended to check my attendance record, and trying to look a little vague, I said, "No, he didn't come in this morning." "Dear God, " I thought, "What if he keeps asking questions? Do I dare lie to him? And, is it illegal to lie to the law?"

"But he was here yesterday," the man persisted. I pretended to check my attendance records again and said, "Yes, he was."

"All day?"

"As far as I know-he didn't check out."

Thankfully, the man left. Days later Irma, the school's cleaning woman, saw me alone after school. A squat, bent-over woman with stringy blonde hair, she labored over a floor that never looked clean. It was a porous brown asphalt tile, and no matter how diligently Irma pushed her mop, nothing ever improved its looks.

She, too, was related to this family in some way-a cousin, perhaps. "I know what ya <u>done</u> for Benjy and his mother," she said, peering over her mop handle.

"I don't know what you mean."

"That's OK, it was for the good. I'm <u>for</u> ya." And then she shuffled off.

I stayed away from the shelter because I wanted to be able to say I had not seen Benjy or his mother, should that heavy-set sheriff come stomping into my room again. One time the sheriff's car had followed me partly home from school-until I lost him at the mall. I parked my car in a space where there were no others nearby and then literally ran into the nearest large department store. I didn't go to the ladies' restroom-that was too obvious-I went to the underwear department and tried on bras for at least an hour in the back room. Later, I slipped out, feeling guilty for some reason, looking over my shoulder. Maybe the whole thing was my imagination.

As for Benjy and his mom, I had called the shelter several times, and I knew Kristine and Benjy were worried about where they would go when their month was up. At that time, the longest time allowed in the shelter was one month. I had thought that maybe I could take them into my home, but I quickly rejected that idea. It would put my family at risk, if that man should follow me home from school and then go on a killing rampage. Also, I had just learned that my brother in another state had lost yet another job and was in danger of being evicted. I might need to take him and his wife and baby into our house.

A friend of mine, in whom I had confided, insisted that she would take this family, Benjy and Kristine, into her house. A tough woman, she was not afraid of any abusive husband who might show up. Kristine and Benjy stayed with my friend for only a few days. Happily, Kristine got a job in a factory and found a trailer to live in. I began to stop looking over my shoulder for a green truck.

Several months after this time, the principal called me into the office. "I'm sure you know where the Crawford woman and her son went."

"Why do you think that?" I quaked.

"Because Benjy is enrolled in a school in your town. They sent for his records."

"Why do schools have to do that?" I wondered silently. "Didn't she warn them that they must not be found? Why didn't they change their names or something?"

"It's a pretty big town," I answered. "I haven't seen them since the last day he was here." I wasn't really lying-I had talked to them several times but I hadn't seen them.

He smiled. "Well, if you do happen to see them, tell her that her husband, Sam, has had a stroke. He won't be hurting her anymore."

I did get the word to Kristine, and I heard later that she returned and took care of Sam in his final days. That way she was able to get his insurance and the house. Her son told me that he was disappointed in his mother for going back, even if Sam was paralyzed and no longer a threat. Benjy went to live with relatives in another state. He wrote me a few times from Alabama, telling me in one letter, why he felt compelled to leave. "I got my stepfather's hunting rifle. I even had it loaded. I wanted to kill him so bad. But like my mom said, 'I would be the one in jail for the rest of my life.'" Benjy never did improve his spelling.

Homeless is Just a Landlord Away

Sometimes the disposition of the landlord determines whether or not a person becomes homeless. Before I did counseling at the homeless shelters, while I still was teaching, I worked in the summer for an agency organized to help individuals who were almost homeless. Persons who found themselves facing eviction or those threatened with having their utilities turned off could come in for an interview. It was an umbrella agency, and its purpose was to help individuals get connected with services, such as food stamps, for which they might qualify. Some people did not know that their low income qualified them for services. Other people might have an income above the poverty level, but if they had some mitigating circumstance, such as a temporary illness, they might get help with a utility bill. At certain times, there was Federal money to provide up to one month's rent, but getting it was not easy.

To qualify for rent money to prevent eviction, the person had to have documented why he or she fell behind in the rent. In case of illness, there might have to be copies of hospital bills or a doctor's statement. There also had to be a letter from the landlord stating that the tenants were going to be thrown out because they were behind in rent. The person also had to have some sort of proof that his or her financial situation was going to get better. For example, a man who was laid off from a job had to bring proof that he was indeed terminated. The man could not have quit voluntarily; he had to have been laid off. In addition, the man had to prove that he had the promise of another job in the near future. This scenario was not unusual for construction workers; they would finish one building project and were then unemployed for short periods before the next one began. Such a worker, however, could only get help with rent one time.

The reasoning behind all this documentation was to prevent subsidizing someone who was going to be in the same predicament the next month. It was considered pointless to pay someone's rent for one month if the person could not find the resources to pay his or her way the following month.

The only time I regretted all these requirements was when I worked with the elderly. More than one elderly widow living on social security came in to say that her electricity was turned off in her trailer and the summer heat made it impossible to stay there. The elderly person on a fixed income could not promise that she would have enough money for the electric bill next month. Although some government funds existed for energy, they were never sufficient for all who applied. This woman did not qualify for anything from our agency, but she did get a free fan. In cases like this, we referred the individuals to the church charities, generally less stringent in their rules. Often they gave money to individuals turned down by our agency. In a health emergency, the woman might stay at a homeless shelter until the weather and her trailer cooled down. When I went to the shelters the following year, I counseled a young mother who owned a trailer but stayed in the shelter while she saved enough to get her utilities turned on.

The agency's policy was not to give deposits for utilities. The reason for this rule was to prevent unscrupulous persons from getting deposits to start utilities and then moving suddenly in order to collect the cash refund on the deposits. This type of fraud caused the agency to take a hard line against providing deposits. Therefore, as a counselor, I tried to help people avoid getting the utilities turned off in the first place. In at least one case, I suggested that the family use their grocery money to pay the electric bill and then go to the food bank for groceries. Eligible families could visit the food bank once every six months. There were also two churches serving one meal a day, no questions asked.

The same assumption was true for eviction. Once a person became totally homeless, he or she had to save up enough money for two months' rent and all the deposits. It was cheaper for clients to stay where they were. And this brings us back to the landlords.

Case One: This landlord was not a total jerk, but he was a jerk: Clients: Leonard, 25, and Marie,

22, and two children, aged one and two. Race: Caucasian:

It was a rainy Friday afternoon, and no one was in the office except me when a very-soggy Leonard, Marie, and two crying babies came in.

"Oh great," I thought. "And I had hoped I might go home early." I gave the babies crackers and juice and settled down to hear their story and write up their application for help.

"I'm glad you gave them something to eat," Leonard told me. "We haven't eaten all day."

I made a mental note to tell them about the food bank and the churches that serve meals. "Why not?"

"We were in court," the wife explained. "Our landlord has just evicted us. We were so sure we would win the case. But he won."

The young couple and their children had been renting a two-room garage apartment for only two hundred and fifty dollars a month. It was all they could afford because the man only made $500.00 or $600.00 on a good month. And this had not been a good month.

"Now my husband is not stupid," Marie explained. "He just can't read. He has that word-what do they call it? Dyslexia. All the jobs he can get are physical labor jobs."

"I've been working for a lawn service spreading pine straw," the young man added, "but we don't work when it rains, and it's rained a lot this month."

13

"What caused the problem with the landlord?" I asked.

This young couple had not paid their rent for three months. It was not entirely because of lack of funds.

"The toilet has been broke four months," Leonard continued. "He promised to fix it, but then it turned out there was something wrong with the septic tank and he said he couldn't do nothin' about it."

"It's awful to have two kids and have to go to the bathroom out in the weeds—sometimes we went to the filling station or the laundromat, but that's no way to live," Marie ventured. "I called the Health Department on him and they came out and said he was out of compliance, but he still didn't do anything".

"So we told him we wouldn't pay no rent until he fixed the toilet, and we didn't and he didn't."

"And he took you to court. What did the judge say?

"We were so sure we would win because we had the letter from the Health Department in our favor. But the judge said the legally correct thing to do was for us hire someone to fix the toilet and then take that bill out of the rent. That would have been legal, and the landlord couldn't have put us out."

"But the fact that we didn't pay rent for three months was a breach of contract, and that gave him the right to put us out today."

At this point Marie began to cry, "He's probably throwing our furniture out in the rain right now, and the one nice thing we had was our bedroom furniture."

I always try to ask potentially homeless clients if they have any family or friends with whom they might live, but this couple had none. Marie's family lived in another state, and they didn't like her husband because they considered him beneath her.

"I had one year of college but quit to get married," she explained. "I took early childhood education, and when the kids are older, I want to be a kindergarten teacher. "

"And your parents think it's Leonard's fault you aren't a teacher."

"Something like that."

Leonard's parents were in town, but lived in a very dilapidated house with absolutely no space. The couple did have one friend who offered to use his truck and help them move their furniture into his garage.

"Maybe we should leave the furniture in the rain and ask if we could stay in the garage," Leonard suggested.

At this point, I told them I was calling several different homeless shelters and reserving a space for them. Business had been so brisk in the shelters lately that they had been forced to turn people away. I had already called all the private low-rent landlords, and nothing was available under $400.00 per month. This couple could not pay that amount, and our agency's policy would not give them the first month's rent anyway. There was absolutely nothing available before the end of the month, even if they could have afforded to pay. They would need two months' rent. Their low income qualified them for food stamps and for public housing, but the person in charge of public housing had gone for the weekend. I happened to know that other clients had been told that the waiting list was long enough to require an eight-month wait.

As it became evident that their only choice was the homeless shelter, Marie began to bawl louder than her children. "I can't go to one of those awful places," she wailed. "I'm scared of all those awful men."

I tried to reassure her that the men were kept separate from the women and children for sleeping, but she only sobbed harder at the thought of being separated from her husband.

"I should have gone to work myself," she wailed, "but I could only get minimum wage and that wouldn't hardly cover my day care." Marie was one of those mothers who felt that babies were really better off with the mother, and she had hoped to wait until her kids were in kindergarten before she had to get a job. "But I see now that I'll have to do something like work nights at MacDonald's when Leonard is able to keep the kids."

"I know some of the people who run the shelter you're going to," I volunteered, "so if it makes you feel better, I'll go with you and introduce you to everybody and help you get settled in." I also planned to find them something to eat, because it would be past time for the soup kitchen. "I promise you it isn't as bad as you think—and they do have a toilet that works," I tried to joke.

Slightly reassured, they hurried out into the rain to try to rescue their furniture. They were going to meet me at the shelter at 7:00. When I arrived at the shelter, they had not come, but they did call.

"When we got back to the apartment, our landlord had not thrown anything out. "He told us he was sorry to see us go out in the rain and if we wanted we could stay on until we found someplace else. 'Only one thing,' he said. Stop your complaining about the toilet.'"

Marie then went on to say she had learned one lesson. She would have to find some kind of work in the evenings in order to be able to move out someday.

So the landlord, after all, was not a total jerk. Having won the legal right to throw them out, he chose not to do so.   As long as they didn't want to use the toilet.

Case Two: This landlord was a pretty nice guy.

Client: Catherine, Aged 43. Race: Caucasian.

"I am the type of person who always pays my bills on time," she explained. " I'm divorced and have no income except my restaurant job".

Catherine was a waitress at the Waffle House, and she received good benefits for that type of job. She was going to need a hysterectomy, and cancer treatment; the restaurant actually had insurance to cover most of the medical bills. However, her salary would only continue while she was working and she needed to be off work six weeks, according to her doctor.

"I have a few sick days, but not enough," she said, so I'll be at least a month with no income. I may not be able to pay the rent on my apartment, so I came to apply for one month's rent. I don't want to get behind, and I sure don't want to get out of the hospital and have no place to go home to."

Catherine was trying to do everything right by anticipating what she needed to do in advance. However, the system seemed to favor people who were not so punctual about paying bills. In order to qualify for rent money, Catherine had to be already threatened with eviction. I called her landlord and asked him what he intended to do if Catherine were not able to pay her rent.

"I'm a business man; I can't support the whole world," he complained. "But I do feel sorry for this tenant because she's been a good tenant. I can't carry her for a long period, but I'll put off eviction as long as I can."

I then went on to tell him that he might be doing her a favor if he wrote an eviction letter sooner rather than later. "If I had a letter from you today, I could make an application for her," I told him, but he and I then agreed it couldn't be done because she was paid up until the end of the month.

The landlord agreed to stay in touch and cooperate in any way he could. Probably the best favor he could do Catherine was to write an eviction letter on the very first day of the next month (assuming she did not give him the rent.) By this time she would be in the hospital, however, and she worried how she would come back to our agency to fill out all the forms for application.

"I tried to get everything done ahead of time, and now you're telling me I have to wait until I'm practically in the street before anything can be done." Catherine left us feeling frustrated with the red tape, but perhaps consoled a little that some help was available and her landlord was willing to work with us to keep her apartment. All of us hoped that her surgery and treatment would allow her to return to a demanding physical job. I left before Catherine came back, so I never heard how things turned out for her.

Case Three: This landlord was from a hotter climate.

Client: Anita, aged 25. Race: African American

I actually met this client the first week after she landed at the homeless shelter. An attractive and vivacious young woman, she was already talking with law student volunteers about a class action suit against her "landlord from hell."

I knew the landlord as a person who specialized in low-rent property and who seemed to delight in putting tenants out. Anita and her husband had rented a small house from this landlord.

"Jimmy, that's my husband, had a job as cook in an all-night restaurant. He didn't go to work until midnight and came home about nine or ten in the morning. I worked as cashier in another restaurant-I worked lunch through dinner, or some nights I stayed until almost midnight. That's how come I was still asleep when Mr. Meeks, my landlord came in. He had a key to the house-and I know that was his right as a landlord, but don't you think he could have called first? Instead, he just came right up to the bed and stared at me until I woke up.

"Well, I jumped up with a start and screamed out because he scared me out of a sound sleep, so he sort of apologized. 'I just came to fix that dripping faucet you've been complaining about,' he said. Well, I did want that kitchen faucet fixed, so I told him to go on in there and fix it while I got up and got dressed, but he just sat there on the bed and tried to slip his hand under the cover. 'You're very attractive,' he said, 'if you'll sleep with me I'll give you three months' rent.'

"Well, I guess he thought I'd be flattered by the chance to sleep with a white man, a rich white man at that, but I wouldn't of had the ugly old thing if he was the last man left. Still, I didn't want to insult him too bad or he might rape me, so I just acted like it was a big joke, and said, 'Listen, we better not be making these kind of jokes because Jimmy will be home any minute. He might not like your sense of humor. ' I wasn't lying because it already was half past nine.

"Well, Mr. Meeks took the hint and went off to fix the kitchen faucet and it wasn't too long before Jimmy walked in the door. By this time I was dressed, so I walked into the kitchen and made some coffee and got out some sweet rolls. I don't know why I was so nice to Mr. Meeks but I didn't want to let on to Jimmy that anything had happened. He's the jealous type, and no telling what he would do. So, if anything, I acted extra nice to Mr. Meeks and after he left, Jimmy fussed about it "I don't know why you had feed that old goat,' he complained. 'He already gets too much of my money at the end of the month.'

"Well, it's just because he fixed something for a change," I shrugged. I figured I had more to lose than gain by telling what Mr. Meeks had said and done. That house wasn't wonderful but I didn't want to be put out of it. I figured I could handle the old goat, Mr. Meeks, if he tried anything else.

"Well, a few mornings later I decided to get up earlier and get something done before Jimmy got home. I was in the shower when I heard the bathroom door open. All I could think of was that movie, 'Psycho', about the girl who got stabbed in the shower. I just started screaming and screaming and couldn't stop.

"Somehow I must have stopped screaming long enough to hear him explain, 'I just wanted to check your bathroom plumbing,' but as I grabbed a towel, he tried to get close to me and said, 'have you thought any more about the offer I made you?'

" I somehow got past him and through the bathroom door and ran into the living room. I can't really say he tried to stop me because he probably didn't want to get accused of anything. What he wanted was for me to calm down and give him some voluntarily. Well, I still don't know why Jimmy came in early. I don't think he was feeling well. And he sure wasn't feeling any better when he came in the door and found me running around the living room in a towel and Mr. Meeks coming after me. Jimmy got between us and lunged, and I won't repeat what he said, but Mr. Meeks had the good sense to run out the kitchen door and get in his car before Jimmy could grab him or get a gun.

"It took me about an hour to convince Jimmy not to follow Mr. Meeks. It took me another hour to convince him the whole thing wasn't my fault. Jimmy is the type who thinks women who get raped must have been looking for it. But even he could see that I wouldn't have any interest in that ugly old man. We decided the best thing we could do was find another place to live, hopefully before I had to go to work at noon. We took off looking for several hours but didn't find anything. We came back about 11:00 so I could get dressed for work, but guess what? That landlord had us locked out. We were already evicted. We couldn't even break in to get our clothes. If I had been thinking straight I would have gone into work and explained the circumstances—that I couldn't get into my own house to get my uniform or anything, but I was too upset. I just didn't show up for work and when I tried to go there the next day, I'd been fired.

"Jimmy and I looked for a few more places, but we really didn't have the money saved… If we'd been thinking straight we would have gone to the police about Mr. Meeks, but probably they wouldn't have believed us. We decided we would live in the car until we saved enough for a deposit on someplace else. I would sleep in the car at night in the restaurant parking lot while Jimmy worked, and then he would sleep in the daytime while I watched over the car. I also might try to find something to do in the daytime, but it would be hard with no clothes or no place to clean up. Jimmy had clothes provide by his job and he could wash up there so it wasn't so bad for him.

"For me, my life was harder than Jimmy's because I had to sleep with no one watching over me to protect me. Jimmy wouldn't hardly let me leave in the daytime—he was afraid to fall asleep without my watching over him and the car. But at night he was working, and I had to sleep in that car alone. I guess some of the restaurant patrons noticed that I was there every night. One night three of them broke into our car and dragged me off into some woods behind the restaurant. Only one raped me while the others held me, but it was awful. I guess I'm lucky they let me go and I walked back to the parking lot.

"Jimmy's nerves weren't too good anyway. The lack of sleep he got in the car plus the financial loss we suffered had just about pushed him over the edge. When he came out and saw the broken car windows, that really pushed him over the edge. I think he was more upset about the damage to the car than he was about the damage to me. He said it was all my fault, that if I wasn't such a whore, Mr. Meeks wouldn't have put us out in the first place.

"I said, 'I beg your pardon, if I had been a whore we would have still been there and not even paying rent.' After that night I could no longer live with Jimmy, so I came to the homeless shelter."

Anita, for all her problems, was a resilient young woman. Within another week, she had another restaurant job and had found an apartment, which she could share with another woman she met at the homeless shelter. In addition, Anita had met at least two other homeless people who had a grievance against the same landlord, so they were all working with law interns to determine their rights against the "landlord from hell." However, Anita's marriage could not be salvaged.

Case four: This landlord was a guardian angel.

Client: Mr. Snow, aged 74. Race: Caucasian.

I did not actually speak with Mr. Snow. I only saw him in the waiting room. When it was his turn for the interview, his landlady came.

"He's too weak to talk," she explained, "so I'm doing it for him." This landlady explained that Mr. Snow was terminally ill with cancer and had no family. Not only had she not insisted on her rent, this kind-hearted landlady had been driving the elderly gentlemen to his doctor appointments and doing all his errands for him. She came to our agency to get some help, because, financially, all of this was hard on her. "But, whatever happens, I won't desert him-I'm all he has," she said. It was heart-warming to know that not all landlords are from a hotter climate.

Some College Students' Opinions of the Homeless

A college English teacher asked his students to write about their thoughts concerning people who were homeless. To warm up, students brainstormed words that came to mind when they heard the word "homeless." Most of the words were negative, such as "dirty," "lazy," "no-account," "alcoholic," "crazy" and "low-life." A few compassionate souls wanted to know "Why?" or "What could be done?" One student, however, had actually tried to get to know a homeless person.

A shortened version of this student's essay is written below, with his permission:

So many times I have walked past homeless people wondering, "How does one get to that point? What events have led these people to poverty? Do they not have families? What is his or her history?" Just recently, I had a chance to listen to one man's answers to some of these questions. As I walked through the Vietnam Memorial

25

in our nation's capitol, Washington, D.C., just days after the horrific events of September 11, I met a homeless man named Don.

The day was clear, a little chilly, a perfect day that comes before the fall season. I sat down on a park bench to clear my thoughts after reading the names on the memorial. A man approached me, an older man with curly white hair. He had on old army clothing, ripped and worn. He approached me saying, "Good afternoon, sir," and asked me for a few dollars. I started to get up and leave, but something made me reach in my pocket for one dollar. As I gave him the dollar, I was humbled and began to feel compassion. I asked him if he would like to sit and talk. He looked surprised and shocked as I offered my hand and introduced myself. He introduced himself as Don.

We talked for over an hour, about his life and mine. It turned out we were both from Texarkana. This stranger and I had both grown up in the same place. He had grown up in a good family and had done some of the same things I had done as a child. He seemed to enjoy talking about a more pleasant time of his life.

We talked about the recent terrorist attacks. To my surprise, he was more informed about some of these events than my friends my age. As we talked, I began to realize that Don was actually an intelligent person. He had his own good ideas about what he thought the government should do.

He then began to tell me about the eight years he spent in Vietnam. I could see a change in his facial expression as he told me about the many friends he had lost in that war. He told me how hard it was to live a normal life after experiencing such horror for so long. He said, "As ridiculous as it may sound, it is hard to function normally day in and day out without having vivid thoughts about that war. That was one reason," he said, "I had trouble holding a job"' I could only partially understand what he meant, not having had that experience myself. But I have heard people talking that they felt this way after September 11.

This day changed me. I began to see Don as a human being with some of the same feelings and emotions that I have. He was not just a piece of garbage. I now realize that homeless people are individuals, each with his or her own problems, each with his gifts to offer.

At the end of this conversation, I said to Don, "Let me get your phone number-I'll give you a call next time I'm in town." Then I remembered- he had no home and no phone. Instead I said, "Maybe I'll see you again-and we can get a cup of coffee."

"That would be good," he said with a chuckle. "Someday soon, and I'll buy the coffee."

"I Only Want to be a Person"

In the last story, we read how a college student came to realize that a homeless man was a "real person." We also learned that the homeless man at the Vietnam Memorial was a veteran. A news article in <u>The Atlanta Journal Constitution</u>, (Nov. 10, 1996;A-8) stated that approximately one third of all homeless men were veterans. In the homeless shelter near me, I met at least one man and one woman who were veterans.

The woman, Frances, had been in the Air Force, had been married, and had a two-year-old son. After her divorce, she left the service to take care of her ailing father. Her mother was dead. The father, unfortunately, was an abusive alcoholic and Frances could not bear living with him, especially with a young child in the house. She was able to get her father into a nursing home, but having depleted all her funds, she was staying in the homeless shelter until she could get a job and decide what to do. Frances and her child did not stay in the shelter long. She had enough education and work experience to make a better life somewhere else.

The man, Andy, was a different case. A Navy veteran, he claimed to have earned three medals, only to have them stolen in an Atlanta homeless shelter. Andy was born in a small town in Michigan. He was the second of three children, and when he was four, his mother had a stroke. At this time his father left, returning to Alabama. Andy always felt that he was the one who was made to take care of his mother and the baby brother, even though several female relatives came in to help regularly.

"The other children didn't have to do nothing because they went to school. They had a childhood. I didn't." Andy didn't go to school until he was nine, probably because he may have been useful at home. More than likely, the adults just overlooked him. When the baby brother started school, Andy did too.

"I got put into special education because I didn't know nothing," he said. "But later I worked my way out of it." Andy actually graduated and went to a Tech School in Detroit. Around this time, his mother died and the other children moved on.

Andy was able to get into the Navy and was actually deployed in the Persian Gulf War. "I was terrified the whole time," he says of his war experience, "but I did what I was told and I got three medals." Andy did not get along well with some of the other sailors. "I had a girlfriend I was going to marry when I got out," he said. "But her family looked down on me and she broke up with me. After that experience, I wasn't in a hurry to get another girlfriend. But the other guys called me 'gay' because I didn't want to go pick up girls at bars. I guess I have always been a private person-I stay to myself."

After Andy got out of the service, he was in the Reserves one year. But something happened. He was taken to the state hospital and diagnosed as paranoid schizophrenic. Around this time his father died, and Andy really did not know where his brothers were. " At first they said I just had post-traumatic stress disorder," he said. "But when I didn't get better, they said it was Schizophrenia."

After his release, Andy tried to work but he got off his medicine and the same thing happened again. He went back to the mental hospital. "They told me to take my medicine regularly," he said, "but I don't need it now," he told me. In my mind, this was a red flag. Whenever someone has been diagnosed with a specific mental illness and then the person gets off of the medicine, bad things can happen. The social worker at the homeless shelter tries to get people into the Mental Health Center if they need medicine prescribed by a psychiatrist. However, the social worker doesn't work at night. And most of the shelter people I have met who needed this service have told me it takes two months to get an appointment. Could Andy survive that long without a major episode? I spoke with the shelter director, who agreed that Andy needed help as soon as possible.

I talked to Andy a bit more about what he had been doing since getting out of the mental hospital a second time. He had given up trying to hold a job and was living on SSI. He had tried to live in some sort of halfway house for people who had been ill, but, in his own words, "Lydia-she's the one that ran the house I was in-told me to leave. She said I wasn't like the other people. So I started to walk-I thought I would go back to Atlanta where the homeless shelters were, even though the last time I got my medals stolen. I walked for two days and then the police picked me up and brought me here instead." I asked Andy what he hoped for his future. All counselors, sooner or later, tend to ask, "If you could have one wish granted, what would it be?"

Andy looked deep in thought. He then turned his gaze directly on me. "I only want to be a person."

I went back the next night to see Andy, after requesting mental health help for him. I was concerned. He was really not in a mood to talk-was almost incoherent. He said that people in the men's dormitory were spraying poison gases on him. He looked at me as though I might be wanting to spray him with something. "Was he thinking about Agent Orange," I wondered, "or was someone in the shelter spraying for bugs."

I gave up trying to have a conversation with Andy and talked instead to the shelter's director, I asked about the "poison gases" and was told this story: The other men had complained that Andy had a terrible odor about him, especially on his feet. Even though Andy took a shower as was required, he still had an odor. I have read that schizophrenics have a distinctive odor and I had noticed a slightly musty scent as he talked to me. But at least he had had his shoes on when he was with me. I do know that shelters are always asking for donations of clean, white socks because many homeless people have blisters and sores on their feet. Think about it-if you walked from one city to the next-or just around town all day-your feet might not smell so good either. Well, the director told me, after Andy went to bed the other residents began to spray his feet and shoes and around his bed with Lysol, which made him wake up in a fury.

The next day I went back only to find Andy had left He had threatened the residents and the director so was forced to leave. If he had refused to leave voluntarily, they would have called the police-I felt they should have done so anyway. Perhaps the police could have gotten him into mental health. More than likely, though, he would have ended up in jail.

"I did give him a sleeping bag," the director told me. I felt really bad to think that a veteran who earned three medals is on the street somewhere with just a sleeping bag. I remember one of the last coherent thoughts he shared with me, "I only want to be a person."

Margaret: Grandmother and Poet "I wish I was a tree...they aren't homeless."

The careworn woman looked older than her 46 years. "I have arthritis, two bad discs in my spine, and congestive heart failure," she told me. "But the worst problem I have is early-onset Alzheimer's disease. It makes me forget things I'm supposed to do everyday, like show up for my caseworker's appointment. It also makes it hard for me to get a job, and they keep after me here (at the shelter) to go look for work. If I do go out, I can't find my way back."

"But you seem like you have a good memory about things that have happened in your life," I reminded her.

"That's because I write poems and essays in my notebook," she replied.

"It helps me remember things, but now I wonder if that's what I should do.

Some things I'd be better off to forget, like in these poems."

At this point, Margaret showed me this page in her notebook:

Thoughts on Homelessness

The sun is shining down on my face while I am writing. The wind is slightly blowing. I watch the trees as the gentle breeze slowly moves their leaves. .Oh, how I wish I was a tree. Trees don't have broken hearts; trees are not homeless; they do not cry. My favorite flower is the yellow lily. Maybe I'll become a yellow lily. But more likely, I'll just continue along the path meant for me, a life of woes and sadness.

On the next page Margaret showed me a longer poem. "I never published it because I was ashamed," she told me. "But maybe it's time now. I'll let you have it."

No Bed of Roses

Yellow lilies are my favorite flowers
    And I have no bed of roses.
For Rose was the wicked witch
    Who beat me because
The Evil One was raping me.

I remember glimpses of me at two,
　　More prevalent after three;
However, I was beaten by the wicked witch,
　　Because her husband raped me,
While she lay in a drunken stupor from
　　Her homemade wine; her husband "Shine,"
(as he was called), raped my innocent soul.

I begged God Himself to let me die
　　And leave this tortured soul's spirit,
And pull me up to heaven
　　From my tormented body.
No response ever came,
　　Only dirty names and beatings,
And rape.

"Go git me a switch with your bull-head, chicken-head
　　self,
　　You don't mount to nothin', am neva be anythang,
"You-a-whore!" she would shout.

Then when the night shadows came,
　　And darkness was creeping into my room,
　It happened again!
"God, please take me away!
No, I don't want to; leave me alone!"

He puts his hand over my mouth
　　Pulls my gown off my body.
I want to scream!
　　But that would have meant
Another beating, for you see?
I was beaten
Every time my grandfather raped me.

He would jump out of bed if she came near,
  Pull up his clothes and run from the house,
Driving away in the car, leaving me
  To bear the punishment all alone.
My God, I was a baby!

Then one day my tortured soul was set free,
  For God took the wicked witch, my grandmother,
Down into Hell and Judgment Day,
  And today I am haunted by years past,
And fighting ghostly shadows every day.

Sometimes I'm sad; sometimes I'm lonely;
  Is it by choice? Or is it because
I have no bed of roses?

"My father claimed I wasn't his," Margaret told me. "He got my mother pregnant, but then he got ten friends to go to court and say they had been with her. Ironically, that was the same testimony that helped him get me back. At first he said I wasn't his, so my mother got to keep me. She held me in her arms six months or so, but then my grandmother, my father's mother, told him to go claim me; she'd always wanted a girl, and now she wanted her grandchild. So, my father went to court and got the same ten friends to say that they'd slept with my mother and that proved she was a whore. That made the judge declare her an unfit mother, and my grandmother got me. From then until I was about nine, I lived in hell.

"When I was nine, my grandmother died, and like it says in the poem, I was glad. I was sent to my father and

36

stepmother. I thought nothing could be worse than my grandmother's house. In a way, I was right, and in a way, I was wrong.

"Nobody beat me or raped me in my father's house. But there are two kinds of abuse. The first is like what I endured in my grandmother's house. The second kind of abuse is to just be ignored, like you're not a real person. For them, I didn't exist. They didn't want me to exist. And in a way, that was worse than getting molested and all those beatings. There really are two ways to abuse children. And, in a way, the second way is worse. My father and stepmother pretended I didn't exist for several years. But when I got about twelve, my father just flat out told me to leave. 'You remind me of your mother and I couldn't stand her,' he said. 'I don't want you in this house.'

"This was the beginning of my real life. I went to the streets and the street people became my real family. They were my mother, father, brother and sister. They called me their baby girl. They found me an empty apartment that I could live in for just five dollars a month. The man that owned it had a restaurant, so I washed dishes and got food there. The street people got me beautiful clothes. Don't ask how they got them. They also took up money and took me to the beauty parlor every week. I had the prettiest fancy braids of any girl in high school. Yes, I actually finished high school while living like this.

"I was not a bad student in high school, and later I went to college on a Pell Grant. I studied literature, but I only got to go one year. I got pregnant. And in those days you got married when you were in a family way. My boyfriend's family was from the South and they seemed real nice. I thought they would be the family I didn't have. Well, they were nice, but my husband wasn't. He was meaner than my granddaddy, if that's possible.

"My husband wouldn't let me have my babies alive. When he found out I was pregnant, he would throw me down the stairs or hit me in the stomach until I lost the baby. That happened at least three times, until finally he decided he wanted a son. Well, the baby lived, but it was a girl, and he was so mad he took to slapping me around again. So one day I took a gun and put six bullets in him.

"Well, he was too mean to die. I cursed God because he wasn't dead. The police—they knew what he'd done to me, so they didn't even book me on 'attempted murder' or 'assault with a weapon.' I showed them the records of my hospital bills for all the time he had hurt me. I guess they figured he deserved whatever I did to him. Well, the wretched man lived and even came home for me to nurse him. That was his second mistake. The first was when he beat on me and killed my babies.

"My husband recovered and I was bitter toward God because He didn't make my husband die. I even cursed God. When I shot my husband I was already pregnant with another child. One reason I wanted my husband to die was so this child could live, so I got my wish but I didn't really take any pleasure in the baby's birth. It was a boy. When the baby was six months old, my husband went out to play cards. He was bad about cheating at craps, so one of his buddies put a bullet in him. It was only one shot, but it killed him, and the day and the hour that he died—even down to the exact minute—was one year since I'd tried to kill him. So, don't you see? This was God's way to let me know He hadn't forgotten me. It's as if God said, 'I'll get rid of him for you, but we'll do it My way in My own time.' And if he'd died the first time, I'd have gone to jail and my babies wouldn't have had no mother.

"I worked at a lot of jobs and tried my best to raise my kids, but the neighborhood was too rough. It wasn't unusual for boy-children, when they got about 10 or 12 years old, to beat up their own mothers if their parents tried to discipline them. The first time my boy raised his fist against me, I sort of went crazy. I slammed him up against every wall in the house. My daughter started crying and that made me stop before I did him real harm. I'm not proud of what I did, but he never did anything like that again. I knew I had to get him out of that neighborhood. If we stayed there, he might try something else, and I might kill him if he tried to hit me. I sent him off to the relatives down south and now he is the goodest one of the family. He is some kind of minister, but he doesn't have any use for me. I don't blame him, but it was right I sent him off and got him out of that neighborhood. It was for his own good. Because my daughter stayed there in the neighborhood, she got on drugs. I stayed there because that's where my jobs were, but my daughter went with a man to California.

"After my daughter was in California for about three years, she asked me to come live with her. I was hoping

39

she had gotten off drugs, so I took all the furniture and went to California. I had a car and TV and some pretty nice dishes and stuff. I put it all in my daughter's place because by this time she had a couple of babies. I wanted to make things nice for them. Well, my daughter was still on crack. All she wanted me for was to keep her kids while she ran around and had sex and did drugs. One night she went into labor real early. Her baby was so pitiful; it weighed less than two pounds and it wasn't supposed to live. I went to see the poor thing in the hospital, and there it was –having seizures and heart attacks and all connected to tubes. It was a little girl so I decided to call her Margaret Ann Elizabeth.

I was looking through the glass when her doctor came and stood beside me. "Do you want this child?" he asked. I told him "yes," and he said he would fix the papers so I would be the child's legal guardian. "I can see you're more fit than the mother," he said. Later, when I went to get the baby, he sent home a breathing machine and then he gave me some diapers and lots of baby stuff he must have bought himself.

"'Just in case it lives,' he said. And it was almost like he was crying, like maybe he thought it would be better if the child did not live. But she did. I had to feed her every half-hour, night and day. I had to watch that breathing machine and I had to give her all kinds of medicine, but she got fat and healthy and grew, and she got over that withdrawal from drugs, with the seizures and trembling. I was closer to her than either of my own babies-I don't know why."

I looked across the room where Margaret Ann Elizabeth, age 8, was playing with the other homeless shelter kids.. Like a good little mother, she shepherded the little ones, using her graceful social intelligence to settle their squabbles and make them share the dingy toys.

"She seems very mature and well adjusted for her age," I ventured.

"And smart," Margaret continued. "When my baby- and she is my baby- was about two, the social worker came to see me. 'It's a miracle how you've brought that child around,' she told me. You've done a good job to get her healthy. But I have to tell you this,' that ignorant woman continued,' Your baby won't never read or be worth nothin'-on account of it's a crack baby.'"

"Well, I said I'd show her. That very day I went and bought all those phonics records and tapes and all those little children's books. I force-fed that baby reading just like I had to force-feed her milk when she was two pounds. So, at two years, she learned her letters and by four she could read as good as a first-grade child. She reads two grade levels above her grade now."

I walked over to where the child was playing and asked Margaret Ann Elizabeth to read one of her favorite books to me. She disappeared into the room she shared with her grandmother and brought back <u>The Secret Garden</u>. The reading level was 6.0. She was getting ready to enter fourth grade. After reading a few paragraphs to me and telling me the parts she liked best, she went back to her play. I continued listening to the grandmother.

"I took care of my baby and my daughter's other two children in the same house for several more years. I started to take my baby and leave but I felt sorry for those others. My daughter just got worse and worse. She must have had six or seven babies. One died and at least two got taken away from her while they were still in the hospital. She had three in the house besides my Maragaret Ann Elizabeth, my baby I had legal custody of.

"Meanwhile, my things began to disappear. My daughter sold my TV and stereo for dope. She took my good dishes and some of the furniture. She even stole my car and sold it, and her kids were crying for food half the time. I began to feel hatred for my own daughter, for what she was doing to us all. She went to rehab once or twice but nothing worked. I tried to work a little, but that meant I had to neglect the kids by leaving them alone. And the little bit I earned couldn't feed us all. I realized that the only way we could get some peace was for my daughter to die. I began to plot how I might kill her. I kept a gun under my mattress. For the second time in my life I plotted to kill my own family, and for the second time, the Lord got in my way.

"Here is what I planned to do. I didn't want to just kill my daughter and dump her body in the garbage or some disrespectful place. In spite of how bad she was, I wanted her in some Christian burial place. There was a cemetery across the street. Once when I walked by there, I saw where they kept the shovels in the shed. I would shoot my daughter while she was asleep in the middle of the night and then drag her over there and bury her in that cemetery. *I would get rid of the gun somehow and then just say she never came home. But I had a problem; how would I get her body across the street. Even in the middle of the night there might be some cars on that street. While I was worrying about how I was going to carry out this plan, things kept on getting worse and worse.*

"Well, the welfare workers came and went and they never really knew that Margaret Ann Elizabeth was mine. I don't think they saw her because I had her in kindergarten. One day, a woman showed up and packed up my daughter's other three kids. 'I've finally got foster homes for all three of them. Nobody wants these crack kids, so it wasn't easy.' This woman stopped dead in her tracks when she saw my Margaret Ann Elizabeth."

"'Now where did this one come from?'" she asked. "I was told Tina had three kids, not four.'

"This one's mine and you're not touching her," I said.

"'Well, does she live here?' she wanted to know. 'Cause if she does, she's got to go. This is a crack house, and it's a shame and a disgrace to have children here.'

"I have nothing to do with dope, and I hav legal custody of this child," I told her.

"'Well, you have allowed your daughter to bring crack in the house and it's your fault as much as hers, so your child goes too. But I don't have a home for her today. I'll have to come back tomorrow.'

"Well, in the middle of the night I got up. That woman was supposed to come for my child first thing in the morning. I won't tell you what I had to do to get our bus tickets, but I got them. And I never did hear if that welfare woman showed up the next morning. If she did we were long gone, on the bus to Chicago.

"We stayed in Chicago for awhile and I worked to support Margaret Ann Elizabeth, but then my health started going downhill in that cold climate. The doctor told me if I wanted to get healthy, I should go to a warmer place."

Margaret then told me that she had searched for her husband's relatives who were "much nicer than he ever was," but they either had died or moved away. She also had hoped she might have some kind of relationship with her son who was a minister. He was respectful and polite, but had no interest in being involved. After all, she had been the one who abandoned him.

In spite of all her sorrows, Margaret said that she felt God had not let her live in vain. "I did all sorts of bad things, and twice I tried to murder someone in my family, but God didn't let it happen. He saved my life so that I could save Margaret Ann Elizabeth. If I didn't take care of her, she would have died. And that is why God put me here and let me live. My purpose in life is this child."

<u>Epilogue</u>: Some months later I tried to check up on this woman and her remarkable and intelligent granddaughter. Sadly, I learned that they had been separated. Margaret had begun to believe other people were stealing from her and had been expelled from the shelter for getting into arguments. At the same time, the child services workers had decided that the child needed to be in a foster home, that Margaret was mentally

incompetent (as well as homeless) and could not raise a child. The child, ever resilient, is thriving in a foster home and is in a program to educate gifted children. I do not know how or where the grandmother is doing, but the child she saved is doing well.

"The Other Kids Make Fun of Me"

When I arrived at the shelter one rainy Friday, I was asked to see a young mother who wanted help with her child. Marcia, 23, had two children: a girl of seven and a boy of four. Her problem, she said, was how to control Lily, the seven year old.

"She doesn't like me," said Marcia,"and she wants to get me in trouble. I'm afraid she'll get us kicked out of this shelter and I'll lose both my kids and go back to jail."

"Tell me about it."

Marcia, it seemed, had been sent to jail on a drug charge. During this time, the children stayed with an aunt, who had a nice home and back yard. Before Marcia was arrested, her children had witnessed a terrible event. One of the drug dealers had come to the house and beaten and raped Marcia..

"Timmie was just a baby," she said. "He wouldn't remember. But Lily was three and she saw it all. I think she is scared of me because she saw all that happen. And I think she hates me because I went to jail and left her. That's why she keeps trying to get me in trouble. DFACS is giving me my kids on a trial basis, but I have to prove to them I'm a good mother. I can't do that if Lily keeps acting up.."

My first reaction was "What on earth was DFACS thinking to give the kids back while this woman was still homeless? Why didn't they wait until she got her act together?" But of course I didn't say that out loud.

"Do you have a plan for providing a home for the kids?" I asked. I was thinking that they must be missing the aunt's house and the yard with a swing. "I have a job already," Marcia answered. "But I have to stay here as long as I can to save for the deposit on an apartment. And I won't be able to stay here if Lily doesn't behave." This particular shelter did have some strict rules that the mothers must keep their children under control. With a lot of families packed into a tight place, they could not allow children to be noisy nor could children be allowed to bother other people's belongings.

"What kind of bad things does she do?" I asked.

"She cries," Marcia replied.

"She cries-that's it?" "Poor child," I was thinking. "How she must hate it here." I will admit, I don't have a lot of patience with parents who use drugs. I tend to be intolerant in that department. As counselors, we are not supposed to be judgmental. I'm working on it, but I'm not there yet.

"She cries every morning when she wakes up," Marcia continued. "I think when she looks at me she thinks about that night I was raped and all the other nights bad people were in our house. I think she is afraid some of that stuff will happen again. But it won't. I changed. I'm different now.

"I'll bet," I thought. "I have heard that story before. But at least the woman has some insight," I thought. "Maybe the child does have some kind of post traumatic stress that seeing her mother brings on."

I asked Marcia if she had found out what was troubling the child and she hadn't. I also asked her what she did when her little girl cried.

"She starts to cry every morning when she first wakes up," Marcia continued. ."Some people are still asleep, and even though we have to get up at six, people don't want to be waked up at five or even five thirty. They kick us all out at seven. Anyway, at first when she would wake up and start making that racket, I'd just give her little slaps on the mouth until she shut up."

I swallowed hard. "And did that work?"

"Not really. And the slaps made noise, too. Then one of the other mothers, who was really a pretty nice lady, told me I should stop. She said I was lucky the person in charge of this shelter didn't see me. She told me about this other lady who slapped her kid really hard at breakfast. The kid wouldn't eat or something, so the mother smacked him upside the head so hard he fell out of his chair and got a split lip. The people in charge called the Child Abuse number and the woman went to jail and the kid to foster care. I don't think she ever did get him back."

"Well, after I heard that, I decided I would have to do something else. So now I stuff a pair of socks in her mouth just the minute she wakes up. And now I'm afraid she'll tell on me or some of these people might see me and tell on me. I can't have her crying or else DFACS will say that the kid isn't happy with me and I won't get either of my kids back."

As appalled as I was, I did have some feeling for this woman's dilemma. The shelter demands that the kids be silent and compliant, but the mothers are limited in their options for controlling behavior. The shelter periodically puts on parenting classes, but having taught a few of those myself, I can say that they are mostly helpful for middle class children. "If little Johnny doesn't behave," the popular wisdom goes, "just take his Nintendo, his VCR and his computer away. Send him to his personal room. Or don't let him have all his friends for a sleepover. On the positive side, promise the child a trip to the circus or some special event." These mothers don't have as many options, so they resort to smacking their kids, as they themselves were often smacked, and then they get in trouble with authorities.

"Let me talk to Lily for awhile, and I'll see what's going on. OK?"

If you ask a small child what is bothering him or her, the answer is usually "Nothing" of "I don't know." I usually ask them to draw pictures. Lily liked to work with crayons so soon I asked her to draw me a picture of her family. She complied by drawing a smiling mother and two smiling children. If children are beaten a lot, they might, for example, draw a scowling parent with a great big hand. She did draw herself as small and with no arms, which sometimes indicates a feeling of helplessness, a lack of power on the part of the child. I next asked Lily to draw me the "home you would like to live in if you could live anyplace you liked." Lily drew a house with a child in the swing and a smiling woman watching over the child. I immediately jumped to the wrong conclusion that she must be drawing the aunt's house and the smiling woman was the aunt. However, when I asked Lily to tell me about her picture, she said the house was one she would like to have with her mother and brother and the smiling woman was actually her mother.

After the child had drawn two positive images of her mother, I tried using words. "If you could think of only three words to describe your mother, what would they be?"

"Love. Pretty. Nice."

"It sounds like you really love your mom. Was there ever time you were mad at her? Some children might be mad if their mothers had to go away and leave them."

"Well, I was. But my aunt told me my mother was sick and that when she was well she would come back and get me."

"Are you happy that mother got well and came to get you?"

"Yes."

"Your mother is worried because you cry so much in the morning. Can you tell me why you do that?"

"Oh, it's because I don't want to go to school. The kids on the bus make fun of me and then the kids in my class make fun of me?"

"Did you always hate school?"

"Oh, no, just since I came here to this place. As soon as I get on the bus, the kids start saying I'm homeless and the kids in my class talk about how I live in a homeless shelter."

This child's revelation showed me how we can jump to all the wrong conclusions. I thought her problem was all about the mother, but her crying was more about being teased at school. Of course one might argue that the mother's early neglect made the child more vulnerable to teasing, but the immediate problem was the teasing. I immediately talked with Margaret's granddaughter who rode the same bus and asked her if she suffered teasing from the other children because the bus stopped at the homeless shelter.

"Oh, sure, but I just tell them to shut their mouths-that who I am doesn't depend on what they say." This child was older than Lily and was very bright, but she also was more resilient, perhaps from the close bond she had with her grandmother as a very young child.

Back to Lily's problem, I contacted the school counselor who was aware of the problem. She had already talked to Lily's class about not bullying, but it had not stopped the negative behavior entirely. We decided it might be good to have Lily moved to another class where no one knew her. The problem of the bus remained. School systems expect children to get on the bus where they live. Fortunately, the school system had a social worker who worked only with homeless children. She was able to get permission for Lily to ride another bus which stopped at an apartment building four blocks away. Lily's mother was only too happy to walk her child the four blocks every morning, once she learned that her daughter did not hate her and was not trying to get her in trouble. She was almost overjoyed to hear that her daughter's crying was about some mean kids on the bus, something she might have learned if she had listened instead of stuffing the socks in Lily's mouth.

Some months later I ran into a smiling Marcia and her two smiling kids downtown. She told me enthusiastically that she finally had her own apartment, she still had her job, she was still clean and sober, and DFACS was going to let her keep her kids. Lily no longer cried in the morning. "I don't have to pretend I'm not homeless anymore." she said. I wished them all well.

Selena and Elena: Ages 32 and 12. Mexican American
"I saw that the Virgin Mary was crying."

Elena, 12, was an articulate child with sparkling black eyes and a toothy smile. It was hard to believe that this bubbly young girl had been depressed, even suicidal. In many ways she seemed younger than her 12 years, but her full figure made her appear more sexual, in a naïve way. The shapely figure was in contrast to her innocent chatter and the little-girl hair bow on her silky curls.

"I don't let boys touch my butt," was the first thing she told me.

I wondered why she thought I would think such a thing. Her mother had just asked me to talk to her about her refusal to eat at the soup kitchen. The mother, Selena, was attending college in order to get a temporary teaching certificate. The mother was from Mexico and the father was American. The couple had been living in a small Southern town since the birth of their handicapped child, Selena's younger brother, Alberto.

"I never finished college in Mexico," Selena told me, "but because I speak Spanish, the local high school said they would hire me to teach with a temporary certificate. All I have to get are three courses in education this summer. And then I can get a real certificate later. I have a job in September, but it hasn't been easy. I got a scholarship for my tuition, but no place to live, no way to feed my kids. "

Selena's marriage had been unhappy for a long time, but as a Catholic she had stayed in it. "I didn't want to go home to Mexico because I think I can get more help for Alberto here," she said, referring to her son with muscular dystrophy. "And to be honest-how would I support myself and two kids, one handicapped with a lot of extra bills?" But finally her husband had left and was refusing to pay child support. She decided to take the scholarship and live with a friend and the friend's husband near the college for the summer. In the fall she had the promise of a job and a trailer for herself and her children. But how was she to live through the summer? Her friend, unfortunately, had to work nights and the husband made sexual advances. Selena had ended up slapping the friend's husband, so she and her children were no longer welcome in that household.

Landing in the homeless shelter had not seemed to bother the handicapped youngster, Alberto, but the move had been quite a shock for Elena, who was refusing to eat the food. "I know it's hard on her, standing in line behind all the alcoholics and drug addicts to get something to eat, but I tell her to be grateful because it's God's way of making us appreciate what we have. If we didn't have that food, we wouldn't have anything."

When asked, Elena answered, "Well, of course I don't like the food, because to get it, I have to stand next to all these horrible drunk men, and I'm sure they all want to put their hands on my butt."

This time I wondered aloud why she was so concerned that someone might touch her inappropriately. The bright eyes misted over. "I lost my boyfriend for that reason," she said softly. " And we all got kicked out of Mr. Herrera's house for the very same reason. Mama doesn't let people touch her either."

"Would you like to talk about the boyfriend?"

"He was the most gorgeous thing you ever saw," she said. "He had blond hair and blue eyes and was real tall. I met him at the library. He was in high school and having to do homework because he failed history or something. He came right up to me and said ,"I saw you in here yesterday," and I said, "Yeah, I have to stay in here six hours every day."

"Why six hours?" I wondered. "You must really like to read."

"As a matter of fact, I love to read—but not that much. Mama has to go to class all day—sometimes it's eight hours. She takes Alberto to the free day care that the church runs for homeless kids, but I'm too big for day care and they won't let me stay in the shelter after 7 a.m., not that I would want to hang around that place with those horrible old men. So Mama got my summer reading list for eighth grade and she said, 'You park yourself in that library and don't come out of it until I come get you-is that clear?'

"So I did as mama said for two or three days, and I got halfway through my reading list. Like I said, I love to read, but six hours? So that's why I let Brian talk me into going outside and sitting under a tree for awhile. But first he asked me to come sit back in the corner of the library where no one could see us in this cubby hole thing. And he kissed me."

"I've never been so happy, but of course I didn't say a word to Mama. She would go off on a tangent about the Virgin Mary and all that. And the next day Brian asked me to go across the street and get a coke with him. I think it's only right I went; after all, I didn't even get any lunch those days. The shelter gives us breakfast at 6 a.m. and then boots us out the door. We aren't supposed to show our faces at the kitchen until 5:30 and we can't go to the living room or the beds until 7 p.m."

"The next day Brian and I sneaked off from the library again. He told me he had a friend who lived nearby. When we got there, the friend didn't come to the door but it wasn't locked, so Brian just went on in. I felt kind of weird going in somebody's house when no one was there, but Brian said it was OK. Then he kissed me, and that was weird too, because he put his hands on my chest. Nobody ever told me that was nasty, so I let him do that, but it seemed strange. Then he put his hand on my butt, and I slapped him like Mama slapped Mr. Herrera. And he got mad and called me names, just like Mr. Herrera. About that time another boy came downstairs Brian's friend was there all the time and just hiding out. I think Brian told him what he wanted to do. I started to leave but I couldn't help saying, 'I thought you really liked me.' The friend said,'I guess she wasn't such an easy lay after all,' and I said, 'Is that all you wanted me for?' and he said, 'What else would I want you for, you little wetback slut?'

"I almost got lost going back to the library, and I almost didn't get there before Mama came. All I could think about was, "If I don't let boys do nasty things, then no one will ever like me."

"I'm sure that's not true," I interjected, "I'm sure you have lots of friends back at your school."

"Well, I did, but they won't like me if they find out I live at the homeless shelter. I don't dare write to any of them. " Elena then gave me a hard look with those black eyes. "Do you want to know the worst thing about all that? I kind of liked what Brian did. I knew that was something the Virgin Mary would never approve, not to mention Mama. If I liked doing something bad, that meant I was a bad person. Not only was I a wetback in the homeless shelter, I was a slut besides. So, I had no choice but to kill myself, don't you see?"

Only teenage logic could have seen suicide as such a reasonable and rational choice. Elena continued, "I knew what I had to do. They don't let us have knives at the shelter—I guess a lot of people would kill themselves if they did. They give us plastic spoons and forks. That night the Baptist ladies were cooking us supper. I never liked Baptists much because a Baptist girl once told me I was going to hell, but these Baptist ladies were pretty nice. They weren't very smart, though, because they let me have a knife."

"Mama, Alberto and I were standing in line. The Baptist ladies had cooked up some kind of beef stew. I took my plate, sat down and pretended to start eating. 'Mama, I can't eat this meat-it's too tough,' I said."

"'Now don't start complaining about the. food already,' Mama began. 'If Alberto can chew it, so can you.' Alberto may have weak muscles but he can chew a shoe if he's hungry. "

"Mama, I promise you I'll eat it, but first I have to cut it. I'll just go ask the ladies to borrow their kitchen knife."

"I knew I had to move quickly if I was going to kill myself before Mama and Alberto got to dessert. I slipped into the kitchen and grabbed a knife. I smiled sweetly at the Baptist ladies and promised to bring it right back, but instead of going to the dining room, I slipped downstairs where I wasn't supposed to be. Mama had a statue of the Virgin on her dresser. I felt that was the most suitable place for me to kill myself--while I was praying to the Virgin. I got down on my knees and said some prayers, but I couldn't concentrate because I was worried about the best place to stick the knife—should I put it in my throat or in my heart? I decided on my heart, but where exactly was my heart? I always thought it was on the left side, but once I saw a book that showed it more in the middle. And what if the knife got stuck on my ribs and wouldn't go in my heart? While I was worrying about all this, I kept my eyes still on the Virgin's beautiful china face. I guess I didn't really want to look at the knife—that ugly, sharp thing in my hand. So I stared and stared at the Virgin's face. And I know you think I'm crazy, but the Virgin was weeping. She had real tears that glistened in the evening sun. And all of a sudden I was happy again. The Virgin wanted me to live! She didn't want me to stick that sharp thing in my chest. The Virgin loves me! She really loves me!.

"I can't tell you how joyfully I ran up those stairs. I plopped that knife down in front of those Baptist ladies and thanked them-I started to hug them, but I just went and sat down by Mama and Alberto. They were just starting dessert.

"'I know what you've been up to,' Mama said. My heart froze. How could she know? 'You went outside and dumped your food in the garbage, you ungrateful child. You should thank God you have something to eat at all.'

"I am grateful to God, Mama." And I meant it, more than she could ever know. But then Mama did something kind of strange. 'I sold one of my textbooks we weren't using,' she said. 'I'm going to let you buy some pizza."

Epilogue: When I returned near the end of the summer, Selena was almost finished with her college courses and was looking forward to having a job and a home where she could support Alberto and get him the kind of help he needed. However, she had sent Elena to Mexico to live with her parents because " young girls are better chaperoned there. She won't be able to see any boys without her grandmother present. I love this country," she said, "but there is too much sex going on with young girls."

Howard:
"I still love my first wife..."

"I guess I fall between the cracks," Howard told me. He was a white-haired gentleman with a ruddy complexion, which hinted of his long-term alcohol abuse. Like many of the homeless, he looked older than his 57 years, yet he could still get a twinkle in his faded blue eyes when reminiscing about the past.

"I'm too young for Social Security, but too old to work. At least I think I'm too old to work, but the counselors here-they have no heart. They're going to put me out if I don't go on at least one job interview each day." Howard claimed to have had a stroke, which made walking with a cane a necessity. "I don't see how I'm supposed to walk all over town looking for work when all I can do is limp," he grumbled. "But they still make me fill out my job interview cards and get signatures to prove I went to see all those people. " Howard then grinned mischievously, " But so far my luck's held out---none of them wanted me."

Howard had applied for SSI but had been turned down because doctors felt he should still be able to do some type of employment, even answering a telephone. "I went to the courthouse to appeal that decision," Howard explained " and do you know what that judge had the nerve to say? 'You do not qualify, Mr. Johnson. Being a drunk is not the same as having a disability.'

"Now that's not what both my wives used to say," he sighed . "They thought it was a huge disability—or, at least, they didn't think it was an asset."

Howard is described by at least some of the personnel at the church-run homeless shelter as an "unrepentant sinner." The shelter, understandably, has rules against alcohol or drugs in the shelter. Also, the residents are not supposed to go outside to drink and come in drunk or high at night. Usually a resident is given one stern warning. If there is a second offense, the resident is put out, and he or she cannot apply for readmission until six months has elapsed. Howard had used up his warnings and had been put out during the cold months of winter. Reluctantly, the shelter had readmitted him before the six-month period had elapsed. "It was against my better judgement," the director told me, "but his pastor came and begged for him." However, Howard was not "home free." The administration was determined he was going to go to work.

Looking around the shelter yard, with its mixture of blacks and whites, Howard gave me his view of race.

"Some people have trouble getting along with blacks, but I'm not like that," he said. "The church I belong to is all black. God made us all. My pastor is black. I love my pastor. If it weren't for him, I'd be out in those woods and probably frozen to death. They'd turned me out, you know, but my pastor brought me back—and he said, "'This man needs help.'"

"How did you get to know the pastor?" I asked, wondering how this man came to be a member of the small black church, which was some twenty miles out of town.

"When I got put out of here the last time, I decided to walk to my son's store in the next county."

I wondered how he could limp all those miles on his cane, but thought it wiser to keep my mouth shut.

"My son, we used to call him 'Little Howie,' –he hasn't spoken to me in 15 years, but I guess I thought he might help me when he saw how bad-off I was. His wife, Madge, she's not as bad as he is. If I'd gone to their house, she would have given me something, but no, I made the mistake of going to the store. I waited outside a long time, until I could see he didn't have no more customers; then I started in. Just when I looked at him, he looked up and saw me.

"'Get out of here, you son-of-a-bitch,' he yelled. 'What makes you think you have the right to come in here?'"

"I don't want nothin'," I tried to tell him. "I just want to see how you are."

"'Still the liar, ain't ya?' he said. 'I'm glad you don't want nothin', because that's what you're getting. Well, you wanted to see me; now you've seen me—so go!' He told me to get out or he'd call the sheriff, so I felt I had no choice but to get out. I don't know why that boy turned out so mean. I never did nothin' but spoil him. I guess he blamed me for the divorce, but I swear he used to love me. I got him every toy a kid could want."

At this point, Howard's eyes misted over and continued. "He had the brightest blue eyes, and straight white-blond hair—whitish yellow, just like corn silk. And his mama put him in blue shirts to bring out the blue in those big, old eyes.

"As I said, I didn't want to meet up with the sheriff, so I got out of there and cut down the nearest dirt road. I figured they wouldn't be looking except on the highway. About a mile down that road, I came to a little stone church, and behind it was something like a storage shed. It wasn't exactly the Holiday Inn, but I had to sleep someplace, so that's how I took up residence behind the African Baptist Church.

"The next night they had their Wednesday night prayer meeting, and I decided I may as well go in. It might be better than sitting out in the cold. The folks inside were real nice and they didn't seem to mind I was the only white person there. They even suggested that I use the indoor restroom to wash up-there was just a privy and a pump outside. The next night they had some kind of ladies meeting and the ladies gave me the scraps from their refreshments. I already had a sleeping bag, but one of the ladies brought me an extra blanket.

After Sunday service, I suggested to the reverend that it would be really nice if he would let me sleep in the sanctuary because, after all, the shed floor was concrete, and it was awfully cold, even with the extra blanket they gave me.

"My pastor, he just looked sad and said, 'Howard, I don't mind you sleeping inside the church, but my fire insurance won't be any good if I let you do that.' I was fixing to ask him for some more groceries, but figured I'd wait another day or so. I'd brought some groceries from the shelter, and I also talked my son's clerk (I figured out when his day off was without him seeing me) into giving me a few things like stale crackers or day-old bread. Still, I was getting sort of hungry. Also, it was cold—and bugs! I knew I could keep the spiders and things off me when I was alive, but who will keep them off me when I'm dead? By this time I knew I was going to die in that shed, either from freezing or starving. And I didn't have but one more pint, not enough to keep me warm, you know."

"The next night it was cold and raining and I was hunched up in little ball in the middle of the shed, trying to keep out of the water coming in around the cracks. I saw some headlights outside, and the first thing I knew I was looking up at Brenda, my first wife. In one hand, she had a pot of hot soup, and in the other, a sack of groceries.

"'Get up, you fool, I've brought your dinner,' she said. And you know what? She'd even made cornbread, all buttery and crisp." Howard's eyes began to mist at the thought of that cornbread.

"'I heard by the gossip vine at the beauty parlor that you were out here living in the colored people's church. So, I thought I'd bring you something to eat. But don't you never tell Leroy I was anywhere near you—he'd have a fit if he found out.'" Leroy was a county commissioner and successful businessman. Brenda had been married to Howard for 15 years until she got tired of his drinking. She then married Leroy and lived in a big white house, with columns on the front. She was also the mother of Howie, the now grown –up and hateful son. As soon as she'd handed over the food, she took off in her black Lincoln.

Howard looked me square in the face. "I never saw her face again. But every day or two I'd hear the sound of a car and see some dust in the road-and maybe just the glimpse of a long, black car. And at least twice I found a sack of groceries in the bushes by the church. I knowed it was her because she put in our old can opener—the one I bought her when we first married."

By this time Howard's tears were visible. His face was illuminated as though he was learning some truth for the very first time.

"I still love my first wife," he declared through his tears.

"After awhile it got below freezing and I could hardly wait for Wednesday night prayer meeting, but all too soon it was over. The colored go on a long time with their prayers, but that was fine with me. In fact, I'd made up my mind I wasn't going outside. So when they looked like they was all prayed out, I said loud and clear, 'You have got to stay and pray for me cause I ain't never been saved.'

"Well, the brothers weren't all that enthusiastic and some of the sisters said they had to take their kids home, on account of it was a school night, but my pastor put out his hand and said ,'You-all can go if you have to, but at least the deacons should stay and pray. This man needs to be saved.'

"Well, a good little group stayed, and they prayed up a storm and I was almost saved, but I knew I couldn't get all-the-way saved or I would end up back in that shed. I kept on saying, 'I just don't feel the spirit.' Finally, my pastor said, 'It's all right, Howard, I'm not going to let you go back outdoors.'

"Well, before that, I didn't really know what the spirit was, but you know what? I felt it then. It was like the spirit lit a fire and warmed me up, from the inside to the outside. I really think I was saved. Because my pastor said he wasn't putting me outdoors.

"Then my pastor-he put me in the car and brought me back here to the shelter, and he said," 'You've got to take him—he's a changed man.' And they gave me another chance."

A few weeks later, I was saddened to hear that Howard had been put out again. He'd been drinking and also had made no effort to get a job. No one knew where he'd gone.

Epilogue: A few days later I caught sight of Howard downtown, leaning over a boy with silky yellow-white hair, a little boy about six. A matronly-looking woman, probably the boy's mother, stood to one side. By the time I had crossed the street, Howard was alone, sitting on a bench and holding his head in his hands. He looked utterly dejected. And before I could speak to Howard, a policeman tapped him on the shoulder and said roughly, "Move on—no loitering."

I asked Howard to join me at an outside table in front of a café, where we ordered a cinnamon bun and coffee. "What's been going on with you?" I asked.

Howard brought me up to date on where he'd been. I'd hoped he had found another shelter, perhaps one more suitable for treating alcoholics. But his story was different.

"I found a crack between this old theater building and the sidewalk," he told me. I could crawl in there and it kept me out of the rain we've had. But the police found out about my special place. So now I just move from bench to bench.

"I just saw my grandson for the first time," Howard said suddenly. "Madge, my daughter-in-law, saw me about the same time I saw her. At first I thought my eyes were playing tricks on me, and Little Howie was young again. I saw that yellow-white hair and those dark blue eyes, and it gave me a shock. Madge, my daughter-in-law, told the boy to wait there while she came to speak to me. Like I said before, she's not mean like my son. She said she'd let me see the little grandson if I promised not to tell who I was. So I did as she said. I didn't want her or Petey to get in trouble for speaking to me.

"But when he started to go," and Howard's blue eyes seemed misty again . "the little fellow asked, 'Mama, who is that man?'

"And she said to him. 'Nobody, dear-just someone we used to know."

A year later the newspaper ran an article about a homeless man who was found dead just one block from the shelter. He lay in the weeds, frozen to death. It was Howard.

The Man With No Pants
"All I wanted was to take her TV and a few little things."

In addition to working with an agency to help prevent homelessness, I did volunteer work with a church where a free meal was served each day. Between 100 and 150 people usually came to eat; probably one half were homeless. Occasionally we had college kids who probably had just overspent their budgets, but no proof of need was required. No questions were asked and no one was turned away from what was known as "the Lord's table."

The pastor decided I should wait in the church office, and if he saw someone who needed more than just a meal, he would send that person to me for counseling. On most days I saw one or two during the lunch hour; usually these people were concerned about how to get housing or how to get connected with some other social services. Nothing quite prepared me for the man with no pants.

He actually wore something like boxer shorts, so it wasn't really a case of indecent exposure. Still, it wasn't the kind of attire one would normally wear in public, especially not with a long-sleeved work shirt. He also had no shoes or stockings. All I could think of to say was, "How can I help you?" and then I immediately hoped he didn't think that was I was being provocative by asking a half-dressed man how I might be of service.

"I need a place to live."

"And where did you stay last night?"

"In jail. I just stayed one night and then they put me out about an hour ago.

"And where were you living before jail?" (I wondered if he'd left his pants and shoes in jail.)

"At my girlfriend's apartment. She put me out, too. That's what started all this trouble. My girlfriend took my pants and shoes and threw them out the window. Then when I went downstairs in the yard to get them, she locked the door. Well, the pants and shoes didn't go all the way to the ground. She really just put them on the roof a couple of feet below the window. So while I was in the yard, I looked up and saw her get my pants—and I had my billfold in them-with a coat hanger. She done the same thing with the shoes. Well, of course I had to try to break in. I had just gotten a new construction job and I couldn't show up with no pants or shoes."

"And your girlfriend called the police because you were breaking in? Couldn't you just explain that all you wanted was your pants and shoes?"

"Well, there was this little matter of the restraining order. She had done took out a restraining order and I wasn't supposed to be on the premises."

"I guess that explains some things. Why did you go back there?"

"To get her hi-fi. But I also thought she wanted to make up with me."

"You wanted to steal your girlfriend's hi-fi, and that's why she took out a restraining order. Tell me if I heard you right."

"Well, yeah, I already had took her TV and a few other things. When she and I broke up, I had to start moving things out---so, you know, I took some of my things and some of her things. I already sold them, so I couldn't give her stuff back."

"So you have no pants, shoes or billfold. What are you planning to do?"

"Well, the police let me out with no bail, but I've still got to go to court. As I said, I'm supposed to be starting a new job, but I couldn't go there. So I've got no place to stay-no nothing."

"Where is your family?"

"I've just got a grandmother, but she put me out. I also got a sister but she doesn't talk to me."

"Well, you might have to go to one of the homeless shelters. Have you stayed in one before?"

"Well, as a matter of fact I have, but I can't go back there for six months. They put me out."

"May I ask why?"

"I got into a little argument with this guy, and I hit him with the phone. It didn't hurt him none, but the shelter people didn't like it because I ripped their phone cord out."

By this time I was glancing nervously at the church phone and thinking that maybe it wasn't such a good idea to see this client alone. Obviously, he was addicted to something, and I hoped it wasn't to telephones-used-as-weapons. What this client really wanted was for me to call one of the other shelters to try to get him in. He also wanted me to call the boss of the new job and make a plea for them not to fire him. I could not recommend this client to either place. The shelters have an agreement that if a client is thrown out of one for misbehavior, he or she cannot get in the others until the six-month period is over. As for the job, what boss would want an addicted thief who is also prone to violent behavior?

"Let me ask you something—aren't drugs the real reason you're sitting in the Methodist Church with no pants or shoes? And aren't drugs the real reason you're in so much trouble?"

Surprisingly, he nodded 'yes.' "But I've been kicked out of the rehab center, too."

Jillian Wright

Luckily, there was a new drug rehab program which provided longer-term residence, and Daniel was able to get in. His job, girlfriend, and court date would have to be dealt with after his residential treatment. His lawyer told him that this was the only way he could avoid further legal trouble. But before he left, we did give him vouchers for the Salvation Army clothes closet to get some pants and shoes.

The Armor of God
When you run from the devil, he comes after you."

I never heard whether Daniel, "the man with no pants," was able to overcome his addiction and turn his life around. I do know that homeless people, and other people, for that matter, who have addictions are among the most difficult to help. When I was in private practice, a young mother came to me who was currently living in a treatment center. She felt that her therapy in the center was addressing her addictions, but she wanted to talk with another counselor outside the center about some personal issues. Just when I thought we were getting someplace in counseling, she changed the subject abruptly:

"This is nothing against you," she said, "but I can't hear a word you say. There is not one second of one minute of one hour that I don't think about drugs. It's impossible to concentrate on anything else." I can only imagine the torment she was feeling. This woman had lost her husband, children, and job and had been in jail more than once. She was currently in the addiction center as an alternative to jail. Shortly after she admitted that her every thought was consumed with the desire for drugs, she disappeared. We called the treatment center, her next of kin, anybody who might know where this woman had gone. We never found out. I was sad because I genuinely liked her.

In another instance, when I was a school counselor, a mother came in to talk to me, supposedly about her children, who were pupils in our school. She said she was afraid of what effect that homelessness would have on her children. Her husband was in prison, she said, and she had been living with her mother since she got out of prison. Now, however, her mother had thrown her out and she had nowhere to go.

I sent her to Lena, our school social worker. Later Lena called me back and said nothing could be done. "Because this woman has a criminal record, I can't get her into public housing," she said. "I told her she could go to a homeless shelter in another city, or else she and her kids could live in her car until she got a job and saved up for an apartment. I also suggested she give up her kids to the custody of DFACS but she was not willing to do that."

We talked a little more and then she said, "Well, I hate to think of those kids living in the car, so maybe I'll get her a motel room for one night." I said I would also pay for one night in a motel, and maybe in two days she might have a job or at least a plan for someplace to go.

Two days later the mother was back in my school office, this time disheveled, crying, and begging. "Please, please, please, just give me some money!" Her time at the motel had run out and she had no job. The thought crossed my mind: "So this is what the word 'grovel' means." I had never seen anybody grovel at my feet before.

"We've already paid for two nights' shelter," I told her, "out of our own pockets. We can't keep doing this. You've got to think of someplace you can go, even if it means moving to another city that has a shelter."

The woman stopped groveling. "I do have another friend about fifty miles from here," she said. "I know she'll take me in. But I need money for gas so I can drive there."

I was tempted to hand over gas money. Then maybe I would be rid of her. But I knew better. "Meet me at the Exxon station after school." I said. "I'll fill up your tank."

At four o'clock, I pulled up to her car at Exxon. She had several unsavory-looking characters, people about whom I had heard rumors from my kids who were familiar with drug culture, with her. However, it was broad daylight and other people were around. I was uneasy but not really afraid. I swiped my credit card into the slot, lifted the handle of the pump and started pumping. The gas flow started and then abruptly stopped. She had room for only two gallons.

"You have the smallest gas tank I have ever seen," I said, fixing my gaze on her. She stammered and sputtered something about the gage must have been broken. I never saw any of them again.

A man who seemed to be winning his battle against addiction was Jason, whom I met while counseling at a homeless shelter. Like most people in his situation, he looked older than his 33 years. A recovering crack addict, he had been hired as janitor at the church affiliated with the homeless shelter. However, his employment was dependent upon his continuing to be free from drugs, and unfortunately, he had slipped. In most cases, those who relapse with alcohol or drugs were not allowed to come back to the shelter until a period of six months had elapsed, and they probably would not get another job, but for some reason, Jason had been given another chance.

"I know where I made my mistake," he told me "The first time I came here, I got saved and I dedicated my life to God's will. I thought it was enough that I made a promise to stop using."

To me, it sounded like enough, or at least a good beginning. "So what went wrong?" I asked him.

"When you run from the devil, he comes after you," was Jason's answer.

"I'm not sure I know what you mean.."

"It's not enough to give your life to God. It's not enough to say you'll quit using, even if you mean it. You have to wear the whole armor of God"

I was not entirely unfamiliar with the origin of this phrase, but I was not sure where Jason was going with it. I asked him to explain.

"When you get saved, the devil doesn't like it," Jason explained. "It pisses him off. So he comes after you. It says that in Ephesians 6:12:

For we wrestle not against flesh and blood, but against principalities, against powers, against the rulers of darkness in this world, against spiritual wickedness in high places."

"You see, I knew there were certain streets I couldn't walk on," Jason continued. "They tell us in drug rehab, 'You can't play on the same playground. You can't have the same playmates.' In other words, I had to give up my friends. It hurt I couldn't even walk on the street where I was raised. I can't never look at the house where I was born again. If I speak to my brothers, they'll want me to use. If I go out with the ladies, unless they're church women, they'll think I'm not showing them a good time unless I smoke dope and drink with them.

"You see, I knew all that. And I didn't go to none of those places. I didn't go no place except to church and to work. But the devil didn't give up. It's like a holy war, a spiritual war. The devil wanted my soul. And when I ran from him, he came looking for me.

"A lot of people-even Christians-they don't believe in the devil. Some people believe in God and some even believe in angels, but they say the devil and his demons are just part of someone's imagination. Now, I'm here to tell you-they're real. I know first hand the devil is real.

And the evil one has almost as much power as God-not as much, but almost. And the devil has the power to change form. Didn't he come to Eve as a snake? To me, he took the form of my cousin.

"Like I told you before, I knew better than to go down certain streets in town. I thought if I hung around the church, I was safe. But let me tell you-the devil can come into a church. The devil pursued me into this church. He took on the form of my cousin, who was also my best friend. 'I brought you something,' he told me. 'I brought you a present 'cause I been missing you' so much.' What he really been missing was my money. 'Cause the spirit of the devil was in him. And I gave in and the devil won."

"But you're back now," I protested. "How did you get away from the devil?"

"Here's what I have learned," he told me. "It's all in that chapter of Ephesians 6. Take verses 11 and 13:

Put on the whole armor of God, that ye may be able to stand against the wiles of the devil.

And: Wherefore take unto you the whole armor of God, that ye may be able to withstand in the evil day. And having done all, to stand.

"But in verse 15 it says to have your feet shod with the preparation of the gospel of peace. And I didn't do that. I really didn't know the scripture. I was wearing the helmet of salvation that it talks about in verse 17, but I didn't have the second part, the sword. And the sword the Bible talks about is the word of God.

"So here is how I fight the spiritual war that I'm in. I look in the paper and look at the church news. And I find a Bible study for every night of the week. I might go to the Baptist one night and Church of God the next night. I might go to a black church one night and a white church the next night. But I've got to have the word of God for my sword. Because it's a spiritual war going on."

And for Jason, this war is just as real as any in Iraq or the Middle East.

When I'm Working, It Helps my Mental Health

LaQuita, aged 2o, was the mother of three children, aged six, four, and two. I was particularly concerned about her because she had felt suicidal before coming to the shelter. Her current diagnosis, (in my opinion only because she had not yet been able to get an appointment to mental health), was post-traumatic stress disorder. LaQuita had lived in a trailer adjacent to a trailer where her cousin lived. Both women had three children and were single; they both worked in a chicken plant, only one worked nights and one worked in the daytime. They had an understanding where they "sort of watched" each other's children while the other was at work. In reality, the children slept in their own beds in their own trailer, with the one adult running back and forth to check on them.

One night, after LaQuita had put her own kids to bed and was getting ready to check on the cousin's kids, she saw smoke coming from the other trailer. She ran over to the trailer and tried to get the children out, but only saved one. This child was badly burned but lived. Now, in her nightmares, LaQuita sees the flames coming out of the trailer.

"I hear those kids screaming and I even smell the smoke." She said, "And I hear my cousin saying all the time, inside my head, 'I hate you-I never want to see you again.'"

La Quita soon lost her job at the chicken plant because she was afraid to go outside. She was afraid to leave her children with anybody, for the fear that the same thing might happen to them. And who would she leave them with? Certainly not her cousin.

"She doesn't even speak to me now," LaQuita said. "But if she did, I wouldn't dare leave my kids with her. She might burn them up to get even with me for not saving all of hers."

Without a job, LaQuita could not pay the rent on her trailer. She also did not want to stay there because looking at the burned trailer next door made her depression worse.

After talking to LaQuita for awhile, I realized that she may have been depressed for a long time, not just about the fire. She told me about a rape when she was eight years old.

"My cousin and I were playing in a house with some kids where they had an older brother. He got me in the back room and talked me into having sex. He was about sixteen, twice as old as me. It wasn't a real rape in that I didn't fight him off very hard-but he started tickling me on the floor and then one thing led to another. I didn't know what he was doing-I did not even know what it was that people do to make babies.

"Well, my cousin came in and saw it, and she did know what sex was. She went home and told my mother I was having sex with some boy and even seemed to like it.

"I got the worst beating of my life when I walked in. I had huge black bruises that showed up even on my skin" La Quita had a very dark complexion. "But what hurt worse was my mama kept saying,'You're a whore,' over and over again. From then on, I was looked on as "the whore.' I don't think anything bad ever happened to that boy who raped me.

"I guess I got called a whore so much that I started thinking of myself as one. and by the time I was about 12, I really was a whore. It was who I was. When I was pregnant at 14, my mother threw me out. I stayed with a grandmother for a time, but when I got pregnant with the next one, she threw me out. The same boyfriend was the father of my first two, but he didn't really care for me or the kids. He never really contributed anything to us. Well, the next boy I lived with did care for me a little bit; at least he liked me better than the father of my first two. I had my third child with him, but then he went to prison for selling drugs."

After LaQuita lost her trailer, she tried living with the mother of her last boyfriend, but this did not work out.

"She liked my baby that was her son's, but she resented the other two. She finally told me she would take my baby and give it a good home, 'but I don't want to keep feeding you and those other two.'"

At this point, LaQuita began to cry." So I gave her my baby-I just let her have him. I didn't see how I could feed him." LaQuita and her oldest two children now lived at the shelter. She was waiting to get help with her mental health issues and to try to find a job.

The next week when I saw LaQuita, her mood was much brighter. There was a new daycare center which had opened behind a church. A bright and cheerful place, its purpose was to serve the children of homeless people six years old and younger. Even though LaQuita had been afraid to leave her children anywhere while she looked for work, she was reassured by this bright, happy place. "It looked really safe," she said.

LaQuita had already started a job at Wendy's fast food restaurant, which she thought was much better than the chicken plant. "But I'm going to start working on my GED," she said,"I know that I can never make enough to support my kids at Wendy's, so if I get more training, I might get something better."

I commented on how well LaQuita looked. I had been so sure she needed anti-depressants, but now I wasn't sure.

"I am feeling better," she said. "Working is good for my mental health."

I wish I could say that LaQuita's story had a happy ending. When I went to see her again, I heard that her boyfriend had gotten out of prison and she went back to him. Maybe, for her, that was a happy ending. I have no way of knowing. That's the problem with counseling people in transient settings. You begin to see progress and then they're gone.

"If I Have My Baby Here, Can I Keep It?"

One day I was asked to see a family that had just arrived at the shelter. They had been in public housing but were required to leave because of some misunderstanding about a bill. We talked for a while about what could be done to pay the bill and get them back into housing, but it would take time. The mother then asked me to counsel her fifteen-year-old daughter who was just about to give birth and was having a lot of anxiety.

"Is the father of your child involved?"

He actually was. He had been taking her to doctor appointments.

"How do you feel about him? Do you see him and yourself as a couple who might raise this child together?" She didn't know.

"Does he have a home where you-all might live? Does he have a job?"

"She's too young to get married," her mother interjected.

"How is it?" I thought, "that the girl and her mother think she is too young to get married, but she wasn't too young to have sex, and they see no problem with her taking on the responsibility of a child to raise?"

"What is it about this birth that is worrying you the most?"

"I'm afraid someone will say I can't keep my baby because I'm homeless. If I have my baby here, will they let me keep it?"

I honestly didn't know what the policy was. I knew that DFACS did not automatically take children away because the mother was unmarried and homeless. This shelter was already full of such children. But what about a newborn? Would it be safe here? I might have my personal opinion as to where this child should live, but I kept my mouth shut.

"I will find out what the policy is about newborns and get back to you."

The answer was, "Yes, she could keep her baby if it was born at the shelter. More than likely, she would have to go to the hospital to have it, but she could bring it back to the shelter the very next day."

"She can drop it tomorrow and we'll keep both of them," said Tim, the director for the men's section.

"You know, that's what I did," volunteered Sharon, a young mother of a seventeen-month-old daughter. Sharon, although not quite 20, was employed on the woman's side to check women in, make sure they had clean linens, be sure their area was clean when they left and so on. It seemed like a big responsibility for a girl her age, but it gave her and her daughter a place to live and eat, plus a very small stipend.

The following week Tim told me that Sharon wanted to talk to me about something really personal. She had already talked with him about what was bothering her. .(The fifteen-year-old I had come to see had not had her baby,but she and her mother and sisters had been able to get back into public housing.)

Sharon and I moved into the corner of the living area where she could keep an eye on her adorable toddler. Blonde and blue-eyed, with ringlets of curls and chubby cheeks, little April was the darling of the homeless shelter. Hardened and streetwise men and women, many who had been forbidden to see their own children or grandchildren, made a fuss over this angelic little cherub who toddled about and held out her arms to the ugliest derelict.

"She's spoiled rotten," complained Sharon. "I have no control over her."

"It must be very hard to raise a child in such a public place," I ventured. I wondered how they came to be here.

"My mother died when I was small. My dad married again and I didn't get along with my step mom. I guess I was rebellious. They tried to stop me from seeing my boyfriend when I was a senior in high school. So, as soon as I graduated, I left town with him and moved to South

Carolina where he had a job. At first I liked living with him, but it didn't take long for me to realize that I was not first in his affections. He would rather go out with his male friends than spend time with me.

"Well, I was careless about birth control because I thought a baby would settle him down-make us more like a real family. I guess I never felt like part of a real family after losing my mom, and I thought if I was a mother I would feel part of a family."

"But it didn't work out that way? I guess your boyfriend wasn't pleased?"

"That is the understatement of the year. When I told him I was pregnant, he kicked me in the stomach and threw me down the stairs!" (Sharon is not the first homeless mother who told me about being kicked in the stomach and/or thrown down the stairs.)

"It was a miracle I didn't miscarry. I had to get away from him to save my baby's life-and maybe even my own life."

"I guess you thought you couldn't go home."

"My dad and step mom would just say I should have listened to them. I didn't want to hear their lectures. So I came over here to my grandmother."

"And that didn't work out?"

"My grandmother was great. But she said I could just stay until the baby was born. Her apartment was not set up for a baby." Sharon laughed ruefully. "I suspect what she really meant was that her nerves were not set up for a baby. She is pretty old, and not in the best of health."

"So how did you get here?"

"One day, on the spur of the moment, I decided to go to church. It just happened to be the church that runs this shelter and I just happened to look at the church bulletin board and see an ad for this job. I thought it was the answer for a place to live where I wouldn't have to leave my baby while I worked long hours somewhere."

So Sharon left her grandmother's house, moved to the shelter a few days before her delivery to learn the job, and after one day in the hospital, she was back at the shelter ready to work.

"No, April, NO!" Sharon yelled, as her baby started out the screen door.

"Come here. Come here NOW," demanded Sharon. The baby giggled and pushed the door open wider. She was already outside, when Sharon leaped across the room, swooped the baby up, smacked her diapered bottom and stood her in the corner.

"You WILL obey me if it's the last thing you do!"

The baby whimpered and an older woman glared at Sharon. The younger mothers, those who had babies or toddlers themselves, seemed to approve. If they had to control their kids, then Sharon should control hers, too. They thought she was way too young to be the boss of this place, and what kind a leader was she, anyway, if she couldn't even control her own kid? The older woman made soothing noises to baby April. "That's OK, honey, you're mama's just mean."

I repeated, "It must be very hard to raise a child with everybody watching."

"That's why I needed to talk to you," whispered Sharon, as she turned aside from the other women's stares. "I talked to Tim, (who was actually one of her bosses,) about the troubles I was having with April. I feel like I'm not qualified to do anything if I can't even control a one-year-old child."

Tim had told her that yes, she should control her child, if only to set a good example for the other mothers, because children had to be under strict control in this environment. The shelter rules condoned spanking, but not to extent the child was endangered. The state law said that spanking was legal if no bruises or injuries resulted. If mothers crossed the line into abuse, they would be reported. The mother who had slapped her child at the breakfast table until he fell off the chair ended up in jail. So Tim had cautioned Sharon not to use excessive force when disciplining April

"I'm sure you would never do anything really abusive," I said.

Sharon lowered her eyes. "I haven't yet," she said, "but I think about it. Whenever she disobeys me, I find myself wanting to hurt her really bad."

"So you feel you baby doesn't respect you?"

She nodded. "And soon nobody else will. Nobody has ever respected my feelings."

"Let's see if we can make sense of this. You risked your life to save your baby's life. You traveled across two states to get away from your boyfriend before he killed your unborn child, and maybe you, too. Then you had to leave your grandmother's apartment because of your baby. And now you are stuck in a low-paying job for 24 hours a day, and it isn't all that much fun. You did this all for the sake of your baby."

She nodded, the tears starting.

"And now the brat isn't even grateful!"

She was able to smile through her tears at my irony. "Tim did tell me that I was expecting too much for her age. He thought maybe you could teach me about child development."

In any of my work with mothers who are abusers or potential abusers, knowledge of child development is one piece of the puzzle. Some mothers do not have a clue what a child is capable of doing at certain age levels. Some will spank a baby for spilling juice or wetting a diaper. One mother I worked with left her ten-year-old son alone for hours while she worked. She expected him to not only stay out of trouble but to clean the house, do the laundry, and fix dinner. She was so furious when even a part of it was left undone, she took a broomstick to the child. This mother eventually lost custody.

Teaching mothers about what to expect at certain ages is part of the puzzle. Sharon was intelligent and eager to learn, so I brought her my college texts on child development and child psychology. We talked about how April's "misbehavior" was not disrespect but was a necessary phase for the chlld to learn independence. But knowledge about children certainly wasn't the only thing needed. There needed to be some safety plans. Sharon was a religious person and really didn't want to hurt her child. We talked about prayer and then some safe ways for her to blow off steam. Perhaps she shouldn't hit her child at all until her feelings were resolved. If she still felt she wanted to hurt her child, she was to tell Tim immediately. He was actually very understanding and would give her a break away from April if she really needed it.

The knowledge about child development and the safety plans were important but we really needed to get to the bottom of why Sharon felt such anger toward her baby.

"I'm so ashamed to have these feelings. I know it's not normal."

I reassured her that her feelings were quite normal for someone who hadn't had enough nurturing herself. "You lost your own mother at an early age, and your step mother didn't fill the void in you heart. You thought your boyfriend would give you the love you were missing, but he let you down. You said you got pregnant so you could be part of a real family, and it didn't happen.

"Nearly every girl who gets pregnant while too young and not married does so to have someone to love. And guess what? Babies can't give us that kind of love. All they want to do is receive love." By this time she had read enough psychology to know that most children aren't capable of deep, unselfish love until they are older-and some never do get it. And children are rarely grateful for their parents until they are grown. That's just the way they are, and it doesn't help us to punish them for it.

It was vitally important for Sharon to get some of her own needs met.

"Have you ever thought what career you would like to have, if you could go to college or tech school?"

"I have always wanted to study graphic arts."

We looked into the local tech school and found that they did have such a program, which she could finish in two years. Moreover, she could leave April at a free day care for homeless kids located at another church. And Tim, ever understanding, would let her take off some hours in the daytime when the residents were gone so that she could take her classes. We had one problem: no money for tuition.

We were scrambling around, trying to find scholarships that Sharon might qualify for, when her future took a different turn. Her father and step mother showed up. Sharon had made her grandmother promise not to tell them where she was, but the old woman finally broke her promise and told her son where his daughter was. Both Dad and Step mom were horrified to think their daughter was in a homeless shelter, but they were absolutely charmed by the adorable grandchild. They then insisted that Sharon must come home and they would babysit while she went to college.

Sharon agonized over the decision. Would they fall back into their bossy, critical ways? Would they take over the raising of her child, just when she was gaining self confidence about her parenting skills? Would she be able to study graphic arts in their town?

The last question was the easiest. She could study graphic arts in her parents' town, but she couldn't start until the next fall. However, her stepmother knew someone who would hire her in a decent-paying job. With free babysitting, she could afford her own apartment. This would give her a little bit of independence. Dad said he would help with the college classes when the time came. As for her parents "taking over" the baby, I told Sharon,"You're stronger now. You can just tell them nicely when you disagree." I let her keep my child psychology book to prove her knowledge.

The Homeless in Cyberspace and the Militants

In the beginning of this book, I said that it was not a research study. I do not presume to know all the causes and cures of homelessness. For those who want facts, there are some wonderful websites that address homeless issues.

I started by typing "Homeless 2008" into my search engine and ended up with over 100,000 sites. I particularly enjoyed visiting www.thehomelessguy.org. It is a blog site maintained by a person who has been homeless 22 years; he has a laptop. From this site one is put in touch with bloggers, homeless people throughout the United States. Those who did not have laptop computers described their efforts at sneaking into libraries to use the computer. Usually, they got put out because they carried their bedrolls with them and made themselves conspicuous to library personnel. Part of me had to wonder why such creative and resourceful people did not find employment, yet as I looked inside the minds of these people as they described their daily struggles to survive, my belief that the homeless are diverse and unique was reinforced.

Some of the websites are somewhat militant; the homeless people at these sites want to organize to fight for their "rights," the right to sleep on the sidewalk or in the park, the right to panhandle, the right to urinate in public, and do whatever is necessary to survive outside the system. Some websites list cities which are "unfriendly" for the homeless to be. In many places, homeless people can be arrested just for being visible. They are breaking a city ordinance by sleeping outdoors or doing some of the other things mentioned above.

The more militant homeless websites put forth the idea that all other people care about is preserving the downtowns of their cities for business. While I am sympathetic toward people who need to survive, I have mixed feelings about some of the "rights" they demand. I have been accosted by aggressive homeless panhandlers in three different cities.

In my own town, I parked my car in front of my doctor's office in broad daylight and was startled by a scruffy man who had been lurking behind a parked car next to me. He must have known that a number of women would be coming alone to the women's clinic. Some would be pregnant or sick, and because of their vulnerability, they might give him money to be rid of him. He wanted the price of a meal. Since I was familiar with the resources in our town, I told him about two locations where he could get a free meal. This did not please him; he wanted money. He began to argue, but I just kept walking into the doctor's office. People like this give the homeless a bad name.

On another occasion, I was in Houston visiting relatives. I came out of a deli carrying a large sandwich. As I waited for my bus, an obviously homeless man approached me for money. I was not inclined to give him any and said so. He nodded toward my sandwich and said, "You get to eat that nice, delicious sandwich, and I don't have anything to eat." Resigned, I handed him half my sandwich, which he did seem to devour with relish. "You can have the chips, too," I said. "I guess the job market is not so good in Houston?"

The man assured me that he really had been looking for work. I suspect he may have been telling the truth because Houston never fully recovered from the recession of the early eighties. My own brother was still unemployed and was becoming demanding and unreasonable toward those of us family members who wanted to help without encouraging dependence.

On still another occasion I was in Seattle attending an educational conference. At this time, I became afraid of homeless people for the first time. My friends and I were staying in a hotel which was three blocks from the convention center where our meeting was held. We had to walk these three blocks several times each day, and on the way, we were harassed by groups of homeless people-surrounding us, taunting us, wanting our money.

Several times, I attempted to carry on a conversation with these people. I had recently begun counseling homeless people full time, so I was sincerely interested in what services were offered in Seattle. As I inquired about shelters in the area, one man glared at me and announced, "I don't DO shelters!" He probably was the type who wouldn't follow rules. I didn't get to have any extended conversations because my friends were horrified and hustled me on. "We can't believe you would stop to talk to THOSE people," they said.

On my final day in Seattle, I made the mistake of walking back to the hotel alone. I did not really want to deal with hordes of panhandlers so thought I would outsmart them by taking an alternate street. I walked down one street over from the main thoroughfare. It was mainly deserted-free from the hordes of beggars-except one! A large black man was stalking me. Not wanting to show panic, I quickened my pace, but I was no match for his long legs. He sprinted ahead, then turned abruptly to block my path. Thoughts of my friends' warnings went through my mind. "You are so naïve-you think these homeless people are actually nice!"

Although I was afraid, I decided my best strategy was to act unafraid-to pretend I thought this aggressor was a nice, friendly fellow. "OK," I said, knowing I couldn't get past him, "What do you want?"

He actually seemed to relax a bit, with the hint of a smile. "Your money, of course-what else?"

"You and everybody else," I said. "You are the tenth person who has hit me up today. Times must really be hard in Seattle."

"Ten people already stopped you? You're kidding!"

"Yeah, on that other street-those guys are bru. why I came this way."

He seemed almost indignant. "They're jerks," he said, "You give them anything?"

"I didn't have enough money to give ten people something," I said, "so no, I didn't. But since there's just one of you, I guess I can give you something. How much do you need?" I paused a minute and said, looking sympathetic, "I know everyone needs help from time to time."

"Yeah," he said, "times are hard."

"Well, how much do you have to have?"

He looked almost embarrassed. "You can just give me a dollar."

I was never so happy to hand over a dollar. He sprinted away, and I ran to my hotel, as fast as I could move on wobbly knees. After all, he could have taken all my money and my credit cards. Worse yet, he could have had a gun. I didn't think he had a weapon, but he didn't really need one. His huge hands could have snapped my neck like a twig. I wondered why he didn't hurt me or take my entire purse. I'd like to think that I appealed to the humanity in him. I was afraid, but I also saw him as a person. I think he knew that.

Some People are Just Hard-headed

In every classroom there is at least one. In some schools there are five or six in each classroom. I'm talking about hard-headed children. Every teacher knows what I mean. These children sit down when the teacher says, "Stand up" and they stand up when the teacher says, "Sit down." When the teacher says it's time for quiet studying, these children try to see how much noise they can make. These children push and shove to get in the front of the line, they get into fights on the playground, they talk back to adults, they won't share and they don't take turns. They say whatever comes to mind, and it isn't always polite conversation. If they are allowed to use the restroom, they will be sure to flood the toilet or write on the walls. We call these children oppositional defiant (among other things). A psychologist might diagnose: "Conduct disorder."

One child yelled at his teacher, when she tried to correct him, "You can't tell me what to do-you're not my mama!" The teacher rolled her eyes heavenward and said, "Thank you, God." For that she got into trouble with the mama and got reprimanded by the principal for being unprofessional. Another teacher described a child in her room and said, "He would make a good advertisement for birth control. I'm going to put his picture on my bedroom wall to remind me to take my pill" Luckily for her, no one heard--at least not the child, mama, or principal.

Parents of oppositional children often are at a loss about how to deal with their child at home. Some will tell the teacher," I can't do anything with him either. " Or, they might say, "She always was hard-headed." One mother said, "Just beat him-that's what I do." But if a parent or teacher is too harsh in punishing the child, the child will usually act worse to "get even" with the "mean adults." On the other hand, many parents are much too lenient, giving in to the child's every demand; these children do not learn self-control or consideration for other people's needs. They think they are the center of the universe. Sometimes it's really hard to reach a happy medium where discipline is concerned. In addition, some parents are oppositional defiant themselves and their children may inherit the parent's disposition or the child may imitate the aggressive behavior seen in the family or neighborhood.

Also, there are biological causes for "bad" behavior. The child may have a learning disability and feel frustrated because she cannot meet the demands of the parent or teacher. The child may have bi-polar disorder or ADHD. If the child has depression, it shows up as anger. Also, some children may be upset about a divorce or other family problem and will act out to get attention. This behavior may be a cry for help. Often these children can be helped if their problems are addressed and changes are made by the adults in their environments.

Some children, however, never do get over their "attitude problem." These are the children who get kicked out of their high schools because they can't follow rules. Of course we can read about how Thomas Edison got kicked out of school and then went on to invent the light bulb and other wonderful things. There are a few creative, intelligent souls who will eventually do well, even though they march to a different drumbeat. Most, however, end up with low-paid jobs or none at all. It is becoming more and more difficult for a poorly educated person to find work. If the person does get a job, he or she will probably have trouble with the boss-over and over again. Sometimes these people, once they become adults, are diagnosed as having an anti-social personality disorder.

Many mainstream people-like I was before I came to know so many homeless persons- just assume that the homeless are all oppositional defiant and have personality disorders. They feel that these people are getting what they deserve because of their wrong choices and refusal to get along. The man in Seattle who wanted our money, and who told me defiantly, "I don't DO shelters," was no doubt this personality type. I can only imagine why he doesn't DO shelters. He probably would not obey the rules, especially the rules about no alcohol or drugs. After I came back from Seattle, I looked on the internet and found that there are many helpful outreach programs for homeless people there, but unless a person is willing to cooperate, he cannot hope to benefit.

I think it would be safe to assume that a disproportionate number of the homeless people who live on the street-those who prefer to be there instead of in some program to change their lifestyles-could be oppositional. These are the people who are the aggressive panhandlers who frighten away tourists and interfere with businesses. But of all the people I have met, both inside the shelters and in other locations, I would have to say that nine out of ten do not fit this profile of defiance. The people on the street are more visible to the public and also they may have been kicked out of shelters and rehab programs. The ones inside shelters or other programs may be mentally ill, physically disabled, depressed, abused, or just plain poor and out of luck, but I rarely saw a person who was just plain "hard-headed" who was in a shelter participating in some program to improve. I did meet one young lady, however, who was an exception-she definitely fit the mold of "hard-headed."

Her name was Amanda. An attractive woman of 28, she had an eight-year-old son, Billy. Amanda actually had graduated from high school and had some post-secondary training in two areas: medical technology and office management. Her story is as follows:

"I was raised in a respectable, middle-class neighborhood. My mother was a nurse and my father had a business.

We had a comfortable home with all the amenities. I had a twin brother who committed suicide when we were fifteen. I don't know if this did something to my feelings-but I felt that my parents didn't grieve enough. They kept their feelings to themselves. I felt very resentful of them; I thought they just cared about appearances; they were only interested in what the neighbors thought.

Amanda went on to tell how she became rebellious-not so much in school, but in her social life. She liked to dress in a provocative way and she began to date a man who was of mixed racial heritage. Her parents were horrified and forbade her to see this young man. Of course she rebelled and soon became pregnant.

"My parents said I couldn't live at home unless I gave the baby away, so I moved out. I stayed with my boyfriend's parents briefly. They offered to take the baby or help me financially, but I eventually broke off contact with them. I didn't want anybody's parents telling me what to do-mine or anyone else's. I saw a social worker in the hospital and the racist woman had the nerve to tell me.

"You white girls should know better than to get pregnant by someone of another race. The black men just don't want to get married, and once you have a black child, then the white guys won't marry you either."

"This racist woman was worse than my parents. She thought I should give the baby up for adoption. 'Well, I'll show her,'"I thought "I could get married if I wanted to. My boyfriend was actually willing to tie the knot. We got engaged and I made sure everybody knew I was going to marry someone of another race. "

"Why didn't you go through with it?" I asked.

"I don't know-he was nice enough, but I felt smothered. I wanted to be independent-to do my own thing. So I left without letting him know where I was going. I could have had money from him or his parents, but I didn't want them in my life.

"I did have a hard time with food and rent. I never was much of a church- goer, but I found a fundamentalist type church-they just loved sinners, especially unwed mothers. They paid my rent several months, got us groceries-once again, I felt smothered by kindness. They nearly killed me with kindness, so I took off again. If I had stayed around any longer they would have wanted me to convert and join the church or something."

Amanda then told how she moved to another city and worked in a hospital where she could use some of her medical tech training. "My salary wasn't too bad, but the places I could afford to rent were dismal-in a bad area. I didn't want to raise my son in a bad neighborhood. Also, I didn't like my boss at the hospital."

Amanda next chose to live in a small town, but once again, she was disappointed in the neighborhood and the type of house she could afford to rent. She found a job doing office work.

"I was burned out on medical stuff," she said.

"Was this job better for you?" I asked. "How was your relationship with the boss?"

"Well, this time I had a woman boss. I thought I would like her better than that man I had at the hospital.

But all she did was boss me around-she was on my case all day long."

"Tell me about it."

"She kept telling me everything I was doing wrong until I couldn't take it any more. I blew up at her and told her just to fire me and get it over with.

"What she said next surprised me. ' I don't want to fire you. Amanda. I just want you to learn how to do things right. I'm trying to help you. I would like to be your mentor.'

"Well you might think you are my mentor," I yelled back, "but what you really are is my TOR-mentor."

"So that was the end of that job?"

"Right."

"So what do you plan to do next?"

"Oh, I have some good leads-but I would have to move again."

"Do you think you might try to have a low profile around the boss next time-keep things low key, even if you don't agree?"

"I don't see why I should do anything differently; the others were at fault!"

The next time I went to see Amanda and her son at the shelter, she was having an altercation with the shelter's female director, a no-nonsense type of person. It seemed Amanda wanted to call long distance in order to check out jobs in another city, and at that time, long distance calls were not allowed. They may have been at certain times and locations, but residents could not call long distance whenever they wished.

"What kind of place is this-not even to let me use the phone? You want us to work but you won't let us call the places where the jobs are!" (She did have a point.) "This shelter has not been helpful AT ALL! I would be better off if I went outside and slept under a tree."

The director paused. "I don't know how you would do sleeping under a tree—but one more word out of you and you will have the opportunity to find out!"

The long-suffering little boy, Billy, rolled his eyes as if to say, "Here we go again." Not long after that, I heard that Amanda could not resist having the last word and was probably going to sleep under a tree. Unfortunately, her little boy had to go with her

There was one good trait about Amanda. The same independent streak which kept getting her in trouble did keep her off the welfare rolls. "I would never accept 'Aid to Dependent Children'," she told me, "because then DFACS would try to tell me what to do."

Perhaps if I had had time to know Amanda better, I might have discovered that she wasn't just "hard-headed." I suspect that something about the death of her twin and her parents reaction (or their lack of reaction) may have caused Amanda to fear anyone who might want to be close to her. But I won't find out because now she's gone to sleep under a tree.

For Some, There is Life After Homelessness (Sort of)

I have talked with people who were trying to avoid becoming homeless, I have worked with people who were already homeless and living in a shelter, and I have talked (occasionally) to homeless persons living outside of shelters. Currently, I am doing counseling for an agency that provides transitional housing. The goal of the agency is to help families regain a home and some sort of financial stability. A case worker interviews people in shelters, or in rare cases, families who are living with friends or relatives but are in danger of being on the street if their lives don't turn around.

The case worker looks for parents-they must have children to qualify-who are not currently on drugs or alcohol, and who have what it takes to get and keep a job. The people selected must undergo a screening process and be agreeable to following a number of strict rules. They must be willing to set goals which will improve their lives, such as finishing school. Those who did not graduate from high school must be willing to finish the GED; those who have a high school education are encouraged to pursue college or tech school, especially if their level of education is keeping them from a job which could support the family. Clients who have a low-paying job must constantly try to get a better one, and clients who have no job must get one as soon as possible, even a low-paying one. Clients must take good care of the home, usually a HUD house, and be willing to give ten percent of their earnings for their upkeep. This is usually a good bargain, because any other housing would cost them more, especially when upkeep and utilities are factored in. Clients are required to put a certain percent of their earnings into a savings account, so that when they move out, they will have a nest egg.

Taking care of the home involves a rather strict cleaning schedule, such as not leaving dishes in the sink, cleaning the sinks every day, mopping the kitchen at least once a week, and keeping the garbage put out. Bathroom fixtures must always be clean, and the living areas dusted and vacuumed. I'm not sure my housekeeping would meet this standard. The rationale, however, is reasonable. Clients who live in an orderly environment are supposedly able to keep their thoughts and lives more orderly. Learning housekeeping tasks is not that hard, and it can give the client a feeling of pride and accomplishment.

A rule that is harder to follow is the one about who may stay at the house. The client must submit a list of approved visitors, and others may not stay at the house. Single mothers might want their boyfriends to stay in the house, but this is not allowed. The same goes for other relatives who might be down on their luck. In some families, if one member gets access to a home, everyone else in the family wants to move in. These rules can cause friction, but the client must decide whether to move out or say "no" to unauthorized guests. Also, no drugs or alcohol are allowed.

The maximum amount of time a client may live in transitional housing is two years. Clients who are not serious about working on goals, such a finding a job, are asked to leave sooner. Probably half of the clients meet all of their goals. But the majority of clients, even those who did not meet all the goals, are somewhat better off when they leave the program. One woman, for example, left the program when reunited with her estranged family. Her life will probably be better than it was before, even though she did not meet all her goals in the housing program.

My counseling has been done on a contract basis with the agency and has taken place in the clients' transitional homes. Transportation is a problem with many of these families, so I go to them, sometimes with the social worker and sometimes on my own. One day, as I set out to see Juanita, I found myself dreading the visit. Counselors have to be careful to have boundaries around their own feelings, but in this case, I was beginning to absorb Juanita's depression.

An abused wife, Juanita had endured her lot for many years before leaving. Her earliest memories, she recalled, were those of her mother being beaten by her father. Later, when her husband did the same to her, she considered the behavior somewhat "normal." One day, when her husband tried to strangle her, she began to think about leaving. On another day, when he held a gun to her head for hours, she knew she had to get out-if only she could live through that day. She managed to escape with her children to a battered women's shelter. She assumed she was safe because the location of the shelter was secret. Although she talked with several family members on a cell phone, she told no one her exact location.

When Juanita first disappeared, the husband had gone to her parents, friends, brothers and sisters demanding to know where she was. Since she had not told them her location, he got no information and left in a rage. The women in charge at the shelter persuaded Juanita to file charges to have her husband arrested. At first she was afraid, but then told a police chief who knew her family. He promised to arrest the husband, but by this time the man had vacated the home. He took all their belongings and disappeared. Even though her husband was supposedly "gone," Juanita felt she had to stay in hiding. The fact that he was sighted stalking family members put fear in her heart.

One day while Juanita was still hiding, a delivery man brought some supplies to the shelter. To her horror, she recognized him as her husband's cousin. He saw her. The director of the shelter responded quickly, spiriting Juanita away that very night. She was taken to another battered women's shelter in another state. A few weeks after she arrived, she was chosen for transitional housing. After all, she seemed like a good candidate; she was a mother without a criminal record. She had no problem with drugs or alcohol, and she had had a good work record before she decided to run away. She settled into transitional housing and was able to get a job in a restaurant, but things were not going well. She managed to keep her house clean and drag herself to work, but when the social worker tried to get her to do other things, such as finish school, she got angry and refused, or else she would dissolve into tears. The bottom line-Juanita was depressed. She went to a medical doctor and tried three different kinds of anti-depressants, but insisted that none of them helped her.

At this point I was asked to see Juanita. My first diagnostic impression was that she probably had post-traumatic stress disorder, but she denied having any of the symptoms that go with that disorder. Only later, when she began to trust me, did she admit to having vivid nightmares about the things that happened, and if one of the kids startled her, she might run screaming from the house. In taking a family history, Juanita said her mother was always depressed. Did this mean it was an inherited familial depression? Yet Juanita's mother, like Juanita, had been abused, and wouldn't that be enough to make her depressed? Also, Juanita, as a small child, had witnessed the violence against her mother. We are now learning that children who witness domestic violence are very vulnerable to depression in adulthood. To make matters worse, Juanita's husband could only have exacerbated her condition. Juanita's depression did not just come upon her when she was married. She claims to have been bothered by it off and on all her life. Sometimes we call a lifelong depression "dysthymia" but dysthymia is somewhat mild, and Juanita's condition seemed more severe.

In other words, there were a dozen reasons why Juanita should be depressed. I kept trying to pinpoint what kind of depression Juanita had because her medicines weren't working. I went for supervision and asked, "Do you think this person might be bi-polar? She didn't have any "high" to her moods, but some bi-polar people go from "low" to medium and back to "low." The reason I was concerned was because Juanita said one of the anti-depressants made her feel "crazy." Bi-polar people get this reaction sometimes when on a "regular" anti-depressant. My supervisor thought I shouldn't make that judgment until I had "walked beside" her in her depression for a while. When I was counseling people as a student, one supervisor had told me that I had a tendency to "rush my people through their bad feelings too quickly." I didn't want them to stay depressed too long. Maybe I thought it would rub off on me. One of my clients even told me, "You are disgustingly cheerful!" I had been trying to bring some positive thinking to the table.

Essentially, my supervisor thought this woman deserved the dignity of her depression and I should just respect her right to be depressed until she felt ready to come out of it. So for the first three sessions, I said little, except to agree how rotten it was that "she was living in hiding like a criminal when she had done nothing wrong" while her husband was out there free. To be honest, Juanita didn't want to talk much at all, and the silence got rather heavy. We had, of course, talked about suicide, and she assured me that she would never do that to her children. I believed her. But her misery was getting me down.

Most depressions respond best to a combination of the right anti-depressant and cognitive therapy. In cognitive therapy, the counselor tries to "reframe" the client's situation. It's similar to positive thinking, in that you try to get the client to see things in a better light. In Juanita's case, where everything seemed hopeless, it was hard to reframe her situation. To attempt to do so would make me sound like "Pollyanna", or "Little Mary Sunshine," traits that I had been criticized for in the past. I thought about Job in the Bible and how his friends tried to analyze his situation and make it better, but everything they said only made him feel worse.

As I approached my fourth session with Juanita, I thought, "Something has got to change. I have been walking beside her in her depression, and the agency will only have me come eight more sessions. If Juanita doesn't come out of her depression and start meeting her goals for self-improvement, she is likely to be put out of transitional housing." So far, I didn't feel like I had done anything to help. Maybe I should refer her to another therapist.

This day, on an impulse, I had picked a bouquet of daffodils from my yard. One doesn't normally give gifts to counselees, but maybe flowers don't count. As I entered the house with my bouquet, something changed. It was as though the daffodils brought in a ray of sunshine. This is not to say that Juanita did not cry. She had loved her flowers in her previous home, and she always had

had daffodils. She did cry, but her attitude toward me changed. She began to trust me.

I cannot credit her change entirely to the daffodils. I found out in our talking that Juanita had not been compliant with her doses of medications. She was naturally suspicious and did not want to take medications for the mind. Then, when the first anti-depressant made her feel strange, she did not take the others as directed. Noncompliance with medication is not that unusual. Many clients are resistant and will say they are taking the medications when they are not. Still others will take medication for a day or two and think, "Well, this isn't helping," and discontinue. Finally, her doctor convinced her that she needed to take the medication for at least two weeks if she wanted to see any benefit from it. It takes that long to get in a person's system. She did take the medicine as directed for several weeks then, and about the time I showed up with daffodils, her anti-depressant was beginning to work.

Juanita immediately started to do better. Although she had been resisting the social worker's efforts to get her back to school, she started night classes and was surprised to realize that she enjoyed them. "People always told me I was too dumb to finish high school," she confided, "but I really think I'm one of the smarter ones in this class." She was pleased to report that she was helping other ladies learn how to read. On her job, Juanita only made minimum wage and was never given more than 25 hours per week. She had resisted looking for better jobs, but now she was willing to do interviews. Unfortunately, she didn't get any of the jobs, but she was willing to try. One of her problems about filling out applications had less to do with her inadequate schooling than with her eyesight. She needed glasses badly and was now able to get them. She also had been very lonesome for her church, and now was willing to visit several in the area. Transportation was another concern. Some people give old cars to charity as a tax write off. Juanita, who had no car of her own, was given one of these donated cars, but unfortunately, it was not safe. She had to drive to get to work, but was very fearful every time she got in the car. Someone finally donated a safer vehicle, and this helped Juanita's state of mind.

Although the social worker and I both rejoiced about Juanita's progress, we still had some hurdles to overcome. Juanita began what is known as "playing a triangle game" with us. The social worker, whom I'll call Edith, told me, "You are making my job harder. She likes you better than me." Edith was my friend and I knew that the only reason Juanita got irritated with her was the nature of our jobs. Edith's job was to push the client to do things they normally would not want to do, while my job called for me to be more empathetic and understanding. I tried to tell Juanita, "If I was making you do all these things required of the program, and Edith was sitting here being sympathetic, you would be complaining about me to her."

"No, said Juanita,"I'd still like you better. She's a racist."

This threw me for a loop. "I haven't noticed that about her," I protested, but I knew if I defended her too vigorously, Juanita would think, "Those white people are just sticking up for each other." I asked Juanita to tell me a little more how she had come to that conclusion, and though I did not agree with her interpretation, I'm not sure I talked her out of it.

Later, Edith and I formed a plan. I did not tell her she had been accused of being a racist-that would be violating confidentiality-but she already knew Juanita was unhappy with her. It really wasn't fair, because Edith was the type of social worker who would buy things for clients out of her own pocket if the program didn't provide something they needed in the budget. We devised a plan where we would go to see her together, and if we took her anything, such as groceries after her food stamps gave out, it would always be from both of us. Juanita began to see us as a unit, both of us working for her benefit, and by the time my 12 sessions with her came to an end, Juanita had developed a deep affection for Edith. They still keep in touch although Edith has retired.

In a short time, Juanita will graduate from the housing program. Once her depression cleared up, she was a model client, following all rules and working faithfully. I'm sad to say that she still may not "make it" in the real world because she has not found a full time job with benefits. This is where businesses which employ low-level workers are at fault. Most restaurants, discount houses, etc., do not hire employees full time unless the employee is being promoted to a manager's position. If a business hires someone for more than 32 hours, it might have to pay benefits. If two adults in the house are working at least 32 hours, they may be able to survive, but a single parent has a difficult time. Single parents can't make it on minimum wage, even those who get 40 hours of work. There are public housing programs, but units are not always available. Unfortunately, many clients with children do not want to raise their children in "the projects" because of real or perceived crime in these communities. There are several other programs which help low-income people to own their own homes, but the clients must be fully employed and must have debts cleared up to be eligible.

Juanita has a son, Troy, who is graduating from high school. We live in a state where less than half of our African American boys graduate. More go to jail than go to college. Troy not only was a good kid, staying out of trouble and finishing school, but he also wanted to go to college. I was encouraging him to apply for scholarships when finally he told me, "I just need to go to work and help my mom. I know she can't keep up a home on what she can make." I wondered how many middle class boys would set aside their own plans to help a parent.

Epilogue

I don't know what I expected to see as my friend and I parked alongside the old highway and walked carefully back to the bridge, leaning over to peer under it. Certainly not the man with the long white beard. Perhaps I half expected to see the face of my brother. After all, he was with me the last time I was here. Bobby, our friend, was one of the neighbor teens with us that day more than forty years ago, the day we went looking for the man under the bridge.

No face peered up at us. My eyes were desperate to see a sign, perhaps a scrap of tarpaper from that shack of long ago. I have always been the type to want to go back and verify my experiences, to satisfy my own mind that certain dimly-remembered events really happened, that certain vividly-remembered places really existed. We lived in the same house until I was fourteen. For months after we moved, I had dreams of being in "my" house. After several years, we visited our hometown, and I worked up the nerve to knock on the door of the house we had sold and ask permission to look at it. The tenants were most gracious, allowing me to look wherever I wished, but as I entered each room, I became more and more disoriented. The new people had added on a wing; they had changed the colors and textures of walls and floors, as well as the furniture. Nothing at all was familiar. This was definitely not my house!

"There is one area we haven't done over yet," my hosts said apologetically, showing me the small, ugly back hall off the kitchen where the powder room was. As I peeped into the half bath, my mood brightened. Old, faded wallpaper with flamingos was still on the wall of the shabby little space. Once more I was a small child, washing my hands for dinner in the washroom with flamingo wallpaper. This was home, after all. Without those flamingos, the visit would have been a waste. I left satisfied, and I never dreamed of the house again.

On another occasion my mother had taken my brother and me for a holiday in a small resort town in the "hill country" of Texas. We spent the night in an inn, which opened onto a spacious area with a huge, round swimming pool. Our family lived in a town without a single swimming pool, so anytime we kids could get near one, it was a big deal. I was particularly impressed as to how pretty this pool was because it was so big and round. Patrons of the inn could sit and watch the swimmers from the veranda. Many years later, my husband and I were passing through the area on the way to visit relatives further west. Being the queen of nostalgia, I wanted to see the inn and the round pool. The inn was surprisingly much the same as I remembered; although quaint and old fashioned, it had acquired some fame and was therefore kept in good repair. However, in front of the veranda, there was nothing but a wide expanse of grass. Not a trace of the round pool. Perplexed, I began to ask employees at the inn, our waitress at lunch, the manager, the proprietor of the gift shop. None of them knew anything about a pool. Although none of them had been there during my childhood visit, some of them had been working there almost long enough to have seen the pool.

"Maybe you're thinking of another inn," my husband suggested as we headed toward the parking area. "Maybe it was in another town."

Suddenly, I saw the edge of something in the grass. Kneeling, I put my hand on a partially-buried piece of concrete-curved concrete, as in the rim of a pool. Excited, I tried to follow the concrete rim, but it gave out. Either the rest was buried or only a piece of the rim remained. Looking far across the expanse of lawn, I saw another piece, curved in a way that it could havebeen the opposite rim. I tried to follow this other rim, but it also gave out, disappearing under concrete parking spaces.

"This proves it," I chattered excitedly. "There really WAS a round pool. I have NOT lost my mind!" He believed me, or at least said he did.

Now, looking under the bridge, I wanted to see a sign-that there had once been a tarpaper shelter where someone actually lived. The feeling about my brother persisted; how did he get to the point where he could easily be that man under the bridge?

Perhaps it all started when my grandfather saw him playing dolls with me and whipped him for "acting girlie." When we were in high school, a girl called him a name. I had no idea what it meant; I slapped her anyway. There was a failed marriage, a child, a failed career in a bad economy. There was increased drinking. The judge said, "Go to A.A." It didn't happen. There was some jail time. In time, every relative turned against him, including me. I don't want to think about the man I rejected. I prefer to remember the little boy who made lemonade for a beggar and carried it to him in a crystal goblet. There was a fire in an abandoned building. He was believed to have been in it.

Looking down at the weeds and the dirty brown water, we were unable to see any signs of the man under the bridge. Not even a scrap of tarpaper. But then I realized I didn't need a sign to prove the man under the bridge really did exist and still does. His face is in shelters in every city in the United States; his face is the face of the man who froze on a cold night because he wasn't in a shelter; his face is on the nameless forms lying on benches and in parks. His face is the face of the panhandler, both the dangerous and the benign. His or her face is the face of failed relationships and failed systems. With some reluctance and some relief, we turned our backs and drove away.